Dr Jane Little qualified as a doctor in the 1960s, working as a General Practitioner for almost 50 years. She has a vast experience of human nature and is well up to date with the mental, ethnic and psychological problems so many endure. Interests include singing, flute, gardening and writing.

To my husband, Geoffrey, who has encouraged, read and re-read my novel.

Jane Little

RESOLVING DR NICK

AUSTIN MACAULEY PUBLISHERS™

LONDON • CAMBRIDGE • NEW YORK • SHARJAH

A CIP catalogue record for this title is available from the British Library.

ISBN 9781398460607 (Paperback)
ISBN 9781398460614 (ePub e-book)

www.austinmacauley.com

First Published 2022
Austin Macauley Publishers Ltd®
1 Canada Square
Canary Wharf
London
E14 5AA

Prelude

Bruised, abused and emotionally battered, he was bawling at the top of his voice, "I tell yer, I'm not fucking well going. I'm, I'm not! I ain't going to no bleeding farm. I ain't leaving Chrissy! Ever." A slight pause. "Chrissy, Chrissy don't let 'em take me! Let me go!" The voice rose and rose until her ears hurt.

The social worker hoped no one saw her drag this furiously angry small boy down the steps of the Wetlands School. After an hour of futile reasoning, her patience had finally given up. There was no choice, he had to go. The older girl on the top step had stood very still, the tears slowly falling down her cheeks. A much older woman moved to put an arm around her.

The driver, tapping her fingers in annoyance at being kept waiting for so long, had both passenger doors open. The boy, who was perfectly old enough to do it himself, was still kicking when, with clenched teeth, she belted him in, slammed the door and childproofed it. His small battered suitcase had been placed beside him. She breathed a big sigh of relief as she got in beside the driver.

The boy rhythmically kicked the back of her seat, hard. Wisely, she kept her lips tightly shut, doing her utmost to ignore him. North Norfolk was a long way away but he'd had a chain of social workers. He did know her. She had actually volunteered. Having taken so long already, she now needed to move her evening meeting by an hour. It would take at least two hours each way. Trying to reason with the boy had met with nothing but abuse. Knowing his miserable mixed-up life, inside and out, she had endeavoured to tolerate his behaviour.

Nick had been reasonably stable in the 'Home' for almost two years. Once the abuse had been revealed, it had been rapidly closed for good. His previous two foster homes had been terrible mistakes too. The only hope was that this one would be better. Difficult to believe but if only they could handle him, the possibility was there.

His pinched, freckled face under its thatch of red hair was a picture of misery. "I ain't going. I don't want to go to any bloody farm. I want to go with Chrissy." Kick, kick. "I'll run away and find her. As soon as I get there!" He was hysterical and as near tears as it was possible for a small for his age, just ten-year-old could be. Various permutations of this were repeated until too exhausted to keep it up, he sank back in the seat. The social worker had spoken calmly, desperately wishing she could tell him the whole truth. But she was asked to keep it secret. It would all have been so much easier if she could have told him why he was being moved so far from Chrissy. "Nick, I know this is hard but this will be different, I can really promise you. Chrissy will, as you know, be going home in a week or so when her mum is released from prison. It may not be all that much fun for her. You will like being on a farm."

"I won't!" was repeated a few dozen times with increasing volume. He had been on a school outing to a farm once, and,

8

though he could never admit it, the cows and pigs had terrified him. Mercifully, he then fell into an exhausted sleep and there was peace for an hour.

When he woke, Nick made a decision. He would never, ever, speak to anyone again. He reasoned they were getting him away because he had caused too much trouble. They did that. There were dozens of foster homes he could have gone to without taking him away from places he knew. He'd been in quite few.

For the first seven years of his life, he had been in a happy, caring foster home. Madge and Jack had been wonderful. Madge had died. His loss had been almost unbearable. But he still had Jack. Not for long. He would never forget the utter desolation he had felt when a grim-faced Jack had driven him to Wetlands. Told him to get out of the car and just drive off. Jack hadn't uttered a word to him on that short last journey. Not even a goodbye. Now he was truly abandoned.

He had been in an orphanage for six months of age until Madge and Jack had been approved as his foster parents.

The driver glanced in her mirror and sighed with relief. He had woken up but she could see he was lost in his own thoughts, and quiet. Poor kid! After seven happy years, his foster mum had developed breast cancer and died within months of diagnosis.

There had been homes that could not cope with the rebellious, angry, hurt youngster. There were those snooty people who did it because they wanted the extra money paid for difficult kids like him. Like that place they'd put him in. Extra money so their kids could go to posh schools. They made him go to his room all the time. Often, they, especially if they had visitors, made him have his meals upstairs alone.

Took his social worker months to find that out. The Wetlands' Home had been a bit better if you could ignore the chap who took over at night. Nick could bite but it made things worse. At least, for the first time in his life, he had a real friend, Chrissy. She was two years older, much taller and stronger. When the school bullies had taunted him for having red hair and small size, she had rescued him. Chrissy had stood by him when things went wrong. He had loved her with all his being. His red hair had the temper to go with it. She taught him it never helped. Now, again, he had nothing and no one.

He must, he reasoned, have had a mum at some time or other, or at least a relative of some sort. No one would tell him anything. The speed of the car was slowing now, the journey on single-track roads. At times, the darkening trees seemed to close over the car making Nick even more fearful of the future. The mutterings at the front sounded increasingly irritable. Twice, using the Satnav they had to travel long distances to find a turning place. It was almost dark on this November late afternoon when eventually, at the end of a rutted farm track, they arrived. It all had taken so much longer than expected.

The smell and cold air hit him hard as he crawled out of the car. This was awful. A large dog emerged from the lighted doorway of a brightly lit flag stoned passage, followed by a woman. Dogs scared him. He screamed and tried to get back in the car. The social worker, herself tired and angry and needing to return immediately, grabbed his arm and forcibly pushed him towards the door. The dog continued lumbering towards him, Nick recoiled but a very gentle voice said, "Please, don't be afraid. He's a very good friend. He'll never hurt you." The retriever cuddled into his side. Unwillingly pacified, he involuntarily relaxed a little and his arm went down, felt the soft fur and was strangely comforted by the softness. He was so, so tired, and utterly terrified of where he would now live. So far from anything familiar. The same soft voice with its very strange accent lulled him into the house, along with a protective arm around his shoulders. Eventually, left alone with just the quiet voice and the dog, Nick slowly raised his eyes to see a plump woman with her grey hair tied back in a bun, looking exactly like the farmer's wife in his schoolbook. She had the kindest face he had ever seen. She led him along the passageway into the biggest kitchen he had ever seen. The dog never left his side. There was a long wooden scrubbed table in the middle with eight wooden chairs around it, two enormous armchairs on either side of a blazing fire, magazines, knitting, an assortment of everything else scattered around the room and a massive dresser laden with plates of all sizes. But all blue.

The table at one end was covered with food, from sandwiches to scones to chocolate cake. "What would you like to drink? Tea, orange, lemonade or what?"

Nick gritted his teeth remembering he was not to say anything. "Don't mind." He'd nearly decided to keep saying nothing but there was something about her that stopped him. Truth was important to Nick. The voice replied passively, "Then we'll have tea so as I can join you."

As he sat down, the dog moved under his feet, warm and comforting. "Just help yourself, I don't yet know what you like." For a moment, Nick debated whether to keep up his rebellious mood and ignore the food but he found he was hungry. The chocolate cake was too much. He took a large slice waiting to be told he should have bread and butter first.

She didn't. Just sat quietly watching him whilst sipping her own tea. "By the way," she said in the same almost soporific voice with a funny accent, "the dog is called Bonnie. You'd better call me Emma and my man's name's Tom. He'll be in directly. Been out seeing to the milking. But why don't we go and find him when you've finished?" Mesmerised by her voice, and so very tired, he would have agreed to anything.

It was unbelievably dark outside. Emma held a torch in one hand while Nick clung to the other. His inadequate windcheater did not keep out the cold. He'd no idea it could be so dark. He clutched Bonnie's fur as he slipped in his trainers on the wet slabs. As they entered the dimly lit cowshed, he was even grateful for Bonnie's company. The noisy milking machines were just turned off. The noise had frightened him. He then had to walk past cow after cow busily munching hay, with their tails swishing in his direction. They were so, so big and terrifying.

Tom saw them approaching. His voice had that mesmeric softness, too. "I've just about done, lad. Now you must be Nick." He looked intently at the boy, noting the hand anxiously going to and fro along the dog's back.

"Aye, I've been right looking forward to meeting you. I see Bonnie's taken a shiner to you. You must be good with animals!" Despite all his resolves to hate everything and everyone, Nick couldn't help liking the warm smell in the milking parlour, and the look of this thin, short wiry man with the huge smile who came towards him with hand outstretched. They walked back together. Emma put the kettle on for more tea. One look at the boy convinced her, early in the evening as it was, he was dropping with tiredness. "Would you like to come and see your room?"

Dumbly, Nick nodded. The dog followed as they went up the stairs. Nick took a deep breath when he saw his room. It had been prepared for him! Brightly red and white striped wallpaper, a low bed with a black and red checked spread, a desk, armchair, white chest of drawers a little white wardrobe and a huge array of boy's books. He'd never seen anything as good. She suggested he just got into his pyjamas and get into bed. No mention of teeth or washing his neck.

Instead of changing, he fell onto his knees, buried his head in the dog's fur and wept hysterically. All the pent-up misery and anger from the last years poured out. Bonnie gave his face an occasional lick. Emma watched from the doorway, quietly realising Bonnie was the best help at this time. She crept downstairs. After a long while, Nick stopped. He lay down in his bed finding a hot water bottle. Curled himself around it and tried getting to sleep. He must have drifted off into some sort of doze, then suddenly, he sat up ready to scream, scared the man, and with him, the nightmares would come. He was thirsty, and wanted a glass of water. Hoping Tom and Emma had moved to another room, he waited at the top of the stairs listening. No sound reached him. As he opened the kitchen door, he saw they were still there. Tom was talking gently to Emma. Nick froze. He didn't mean to listen, just to work out how to find a glass and some water. But he couldn't help hearing. Emma was sobbing. Tom was patting her shoulder. "Look, lass, I reckon it's too early to tell the lad yet. It gave me quite a turn when he walked towards me. Exactly like her. Poor little lad. What he's been through just because no one knew where he was. That red hair. Exactly like our Mary's. And mine used to be." Emma rested her head on her folded arms on the table while Tom caressed her back.

Nick stood in the doorway, unable to go back or to go on. Tom continued, "Just hope he in't too hurt, like, to learn to love us." Eventually, Nick stepped into the kitchen closing the door behind him. For a very long time, they just stared at him; Emma's tear-stained face, Tom with his mouth open and Nick wildly moving his eyes between them. Tom found his voice first. "How much of that did you hear laddie?" Nick just nodded. He desperately wanted to turn around and rush back to his room but found he couldn't move. After a long pause, Tom spoke, his voice hoarse with emotion. "Well, Lad, I don't quite know how to say this. Me and Em had a little girl and we called her Mary." His voice broke. "She...she looked just like you. She grew up all happy until summer went wrong. We knew she'd had a baby. And she died. We searched for years for you but she'd got a new name, not married but by something called deed poll. But with all the new search engines and suchlike, we got another expert on it and, well, we found you. And, well, here you are."

21 years later

Chapter 1
Nick Meets His Colleagues

August was being particularly hot. Nick parked in an empty space, freshly painted with 'DOCTORS ONLY'. Last time he had seen the premises way back in March, there had been scaffolding and workmen everywhere. It had been impossible to imagine it would be ready for occupation in July. The ground went slowly downhill so there appeared to be only two stories but a clever design had made it three at the back. Plenty of space for patients and staff to park as well. In his limited experience, that was most unusual. He examined the nameplate on the pillar next to the swing doors.

Dr Gerald Masterson MBBS

Dr Maria Skowron MBBS MRCGP DRCOG

Dr Ikbal Chakraburty MBBS MRCGP

Dr Penelope Smith BSc MBBSMRCGP

Dr Suzanne Best MBCHS MRCGP

Dr Chandra Patel MBBS

He hoped he would be on that plate in the not too distant future.

'Dr Nicholas Grovenor MBBS, DRCOG, MRCGP' would look good.

Despite the early hour, it was a relief to leave the sultry heat outside and walk into the cool reception area. "Dr Grovenor, I presume?" The voice came from a diminutive receptionist in a neat navy and white uniform. She spoke from behind a large counter, with the inevitable protective screen in front. He grinned. "I can't really say Dr Livingstone, I presume, can I? Yes, I'm Nick. Good of you all to come in early so I can meet everyone. You are?" She looked up at the smiling face. She liked his immediate informality. Tall, over six foot she guessed, slim, very good looking with his curly red hair cut short, his freckled fresh-looking face and greeny-blue eyes. Dressed in short-sleeved white shirt and fawn trousers, he was carrying his summer weight blue jacket and his smart black doctor's bag. *Just right*, she thought.

"I'm Jose," she answered, "Receptionist, general dogsbody and sorter of problems. I've been here nearly ten years; I know my way about, so do let me know if I can help at any time."

"Thank you, I will remember that."

Lifting the counter, she preceded him along corridors with various nameplates in slots, up a flight of stairs, through a busy looking administrative room into a large area with a coffee machine and cosy armchairs.

An Asian man was waiting, looking anxiously towards the door. He stepped quickly forwards and grasped Nick's hand, pumping it up and down excitedly. "Nick, how great to see you. Golly, how you've grown! I do realise it's a good few years since we last met. Come and meet the others." Ikbal Chakraborty continued, "So sorry to bring you in early but we thought it would be good to meet up before you started looking at the workload!" Ikbal, about 5 feet 6 inches tall, was slim, clean-shaven with a short mass of black wavy hair. He had a smile that spread from ear to ear revealing neat white teeth. Dressed in a smart suit of dove grey with a white shirt and patterned tie, he looked cool despite the warmth of the August day. Nick for a moment, wondered if perhaps he had dressed too informally. A voice sounded from behind them. "Sounds as if you two knew each other better than I had thought."

An older doctor was sitting in a deep armchair, looking from one to the other. "Remember me, Nick? I'm Gerald. We last met in March before I went skiing. Please forgive me for not getting up but I'm still recovering from a skiing accident and sit as much as I can. Ikbal did tell us you'd met at school."

Nick went over to shake his hand. "Yes," he answered, "Ikbal and I met on interview day at school and remained best friends until he was spirited away to live in London. We were somewhere around 16 then. A lot of water has flown under the bridge. He used to be much taller than me." Gerry was in his late 50s with a shock of speckled grey and brown hair, and distinctly on the portly side. At least he was dressed casually, in a bright floral shirt and dark blue trousers. Nick noted the surgical boot and walking sticks and wondered briefly why a man of his age and so overweight kept on skiing. He was about to respond to Gerald when there was an interruption. "And I'm Penny!" He swung around to see a woman who looked to be about the same age as himself. Nick was struck by her immediately. Romance had yet to enter his life but he was always looking for it. For a fleeting second, their eyes met and some sort of understanding passed between them. Probably as a colleague, this was not a good idea. As yet he had no need to complicate his life.

Penny was slim, of medium height with long shapely legs. Her shoulder-length hair was naturally fair and had a very attractive fringe. With the bluest of eyes, she smiled as she shook his hand. She carried herself with confidence and seemed to dominate the room. "It's going to be great to have another doctor. The workload has become near impossible, and with the new building we now have plenty of space." She looked so cool in her simple, navy shift dress. Her upper-class voice was pleasantly musical. No ring on her fingers.

The door burst open and another, slightly older woman came in like a whirlwind. "Sorry to be late but the kids were a pair of little sods this morning. Flatly refused to get up and get dressed. Had to get them to the sitter. Coffee! Must have some, haven't had time yet."

Nick looked around to see who it was. Penny gave a wry smile. "That is Maria Skowron. She keeps us all on our toes."

Maria turned. "Oh, gosh, you must be Nick." With a coffee now in her right hand, she did a rapid change, spilling some of it, before offering a slightly coffee-stained right hand to Nick. "Hello, there," she said briskly, "I'm Maria, and as you've gathered, I'm usually trying to do two things at once. Mainly in the mornings. It gets better with a few coffees as the day goes on. Anyway, great to welcome you here." Nick saw a well-built 40 plus woman in a liberty patterned, flowing floor-length dress and string sandals. She had grey streaked dark curls that fell over her eyes. She pushed the hair back with her fingers making it look even more likely she'd forgotten to brush it that morning. "Don't worry," she said, as if she could read his thoughts, "I'm changing into scrubs as I'm going to see actual patients. Nicer than videos and phones. Getting less of those now and a bit more face to face." He grinned. Decided she was going to be easy to like. Just detected something not entirely happy in her brown eyes. He wondered what all the bonhomie covered up.

Gerry pulled himself up, speaking loudly to be heard over the general chatter and computers firing up a few desks away. "Shall we move into the conference room to explain how we plan Nick's schedule for the next week or so?" There was a movement towards a room next door. Nick found himself juggling bags, jacket and a mug of coffee, being led to a seat by a long table. A large room with three huge windows on the longer side overlooking a narrow backyard, a high fence and a new housing estate beyond. They gathered around. The chairs were padded with blue vinyl and reasonably comfortable. Nick did his best to look relaxed, meanwhile trying to work out where Gerry's slight accent came from. Not Norfolk like Maria's. "Suzanne will be with us very shortly. I've just had a text from her." Gerry spoke, shuffling a pile of papers in front of him. "As I believe you know from our interview, Nick, she and Chandra work together to do a full-time job here. Chandra is very pregnant at the moment, so you will not meet her for a bit." He looked around the table. "And, as you know we've agreed, with Nick, of course, he will take over some of Chandra's workload during his trial period with us." A mousy looking, much older woman dressed in a pretty flowery summer dress, slipped into the vacant chair. She gave Nick a big smile which lit up her rather serious face and mouthed a "Hullo" to him.

"Oh," continued Gerry irritably, "Where's Jane? Nick, she's our practice manager and apart from engineering the move from the town centre to here without a hitch, we need her now."

His iPhone announced a message. "Bother. She's attending to a plumber. Gather there's a problem with the patient's toilet. She's due to looking after Nick this morning to bring him up to date."

Half an hour later, Nick was ensconced in Jane's room tucked into a comfortable armchair. He looked around and saw a pleasant surround in which to manage the place. One door faced the front, another led into the reception area and the third into the corridor leading to the consultation rooms. Instead of the prevailing dove grey paint in the rest of the building, this was a much deeper shade showing up the attractive landscapers on the wall to their best. There were several tall filing cabinets with piles of paper on top. This was the only bit he had seen in the whole building to indicate there had been a recent move. Except for the slight smell of fresh paint everywhere. Her desk held nothing but her computer.

After about ten minutes, Jane arrived looking very calm for one who had been dealing with an urgent problem. She unloaded a chin-high load of boxes before Nick could get to her and help. "It's fine. There's no weight to them. Just thought I'd get rid of them on my way back. Two problems sorted instead of one. Some people do have strange ideas of what can go down a loo!" She seated herself behind her desk and smiled across at Nick. For a moment they took stock of each other. She liked what she saw but wondered why he looked so reserved. He, on his part, saw a slim tall woman in a business-like cream linen suit over a pale blue ruffled blouse. Her dark hair was tightly pulled back into a pleat revealing fine bones, and a complexion that might have been part Asian or even Italian. Her near-black eyes met his greeny ones, each recognising something but neither was sure quite what. Sympathy? "Hello, Nick," her voice was soft and musical with a strong trace of Norfolk, "you've no doubt gathered by now I'm Jane Mitch, the practice manager here. Such a pity you couldn't get back from the Jordon refugee camp in time for the opening barbeque party. You'd have had a chance to meet us all informally. As big gatherings are not exactly encouraged, we kept it to staff, other halves and children. The weather was perfect and so was Gerry's beautiful garden."

Nick responded with a laugh. "How sensible not to have an evening drinks party. They always do run on a bit later than everyone hopes for."

Jane nodded in agreement. "And isn't there always one person who creates a problem? Ah, we'd better get down to business. Before we do, would you forgive a very impertinent question? In fact, I have." Nick gestured for her to continue.

"Firstly, a quickie. Am I right in thinking you were at Postams school here in Mersham? If so, I think you were in the year ahead of me. Ikbal was. I fear your hair gives you away, making you stand out from the crowd. Just I remembered you as rather on the short side."

Nick responded with a huge grin. "Yes, I was very short until about my 17th birthday when I literally shot up." He looked at her thoughtfully. "I have to admit I have no memory of you I can rustle up."

"No, I'm not surprised. I had no outstanding skills or accomplishments and was intensely shy. You stuck out because you accompanied musicals, didn't you?" Nick nodded. "Now my second question does confuse, and even possibly upset me. I have always understood the choice of a new potential partner would be after interviews and a final decision taken by all the partners? But you seem to have just appeared on the scene. I would have expected to have been involved, at least with the advertising." She stopped suddenly and took a long breath. "Oh, I am so sorry," she continued, "I have no business to be satisfying my curiosity by asking you. I should have tackled one of the others but you seemed so easy to ask, and I suppose if I'm honest, I am a little hurt at not having been involved."

Nick sat forward in his armchair, just stopping himself from putting a reassuring arm on hers. "Don't be sorry. It's an easy question to answer and I can well understand what with the move, his accident and everything else Gerry never had the time or thought to tell you. My grandparents are patients here. When I came home from Jordon for a brief stay in March, I realised they were getting older. It's a long story but…but I owe them my life, and I wanted to be near as possible to them in a general practice when I finally came home. Grandma mentioned it to Gerry when he visited her professionally, to see if he had any ideas where I might look for a job. Gerry said not just then, though it might be possible in future but they did need a locum to cover maternity leave later in the year. Gerry got in contact, and I went to see him at his home. End of story. At least no, I guess. Meanwhile you had all discussed the need for a new partner when settled in here. Ikbal had realised who I was, so I sort of came already recommended. If they applied for references they must have been OK, and well, here I am!"

"Ah," Jane said slowly, "that does take the sting out of the tail. I would have known if they had applied for references, so am pretty sure they didn't bother. Now I can see how easily I could have been overlooked. Thank you so much for understanding."

"No problem," said Nick briskly. "Yes, we'd better get on or it will be coffee break time again."

The rest of the morning was spent learning the geography of the building, being introduced to the various nurses, a paramedic, a visiting physio, counsellor, chiropodist and a social worker. Nick was most impressed by the surgery, just hoping he could remember some of what Jane had been telling him.

The patient's waiting area was cleverly arranged with large glass-like plastic alcoves and back to back seating. It all had been designed with real care, the possibility of ongoing Covid-19 at that time being a reality. Not all the consulting rooms had names yet fitted into the slots. One would be his, another when they got a registrar to train and eventually, they hoped the practice would be big enough to attract visiting hospital specialists.

Chapter 2
Family Information

It was amazing how consultations with patients had changed in the short space of time between Nick's qualification and present-day practice. His year and a bit with Medicin Sans Frontiers in Jordon had been very different. He had missed out on a lot of the changes he found when he returned home. Covid-19 had devastated the refugee camp where he worked, adding to the already impossible number of patients needing care. Here in UK, the worst year of the pandemic, with its social distancing, face masks, scrupulous handwashing and the need to always use protective clothing, was already fading a little. Vaccinations had improved month on month keeping people less vulnerable to the disease. Face masks were still used by many. A number of interactions were still by telephone or video link. What else, he wondered, will have changed forever when it was finally all over? If it ever was.

A few days later, he spent the afternoon with Gerry, listening to him doing telephone and video consultations, talking through morning visits made by paramedics and practice nurses, and arranging appointments for those needing to be seen. Nick had not quite realised how highly trained the practice nurses and paramedics were. He was surprised to see how much successful visiting they did, and how truly expert they were.

Nick knew he had a lot to learn, not least in finding his way rapidly around the computer system in order to avoid wasting time. It had been a long three years since his general practice training. After his two years in a not particularly good GP training practice in Croydon, he had changed direction. He had started to train as an obstetrician and gynaecologist. After another two years, he had decided it was not for him. Having read there was a shortage of obstetrically trained doctors he applied, was accepted and spent time in the refugee camp giving him a gap in which to make a final, right decision. It was, he decided, to be general practice with its whole diversity of medicine and a chance to follow patients through.

Gerry was about to send Nick home thinking he'd had rather a boring day when he hesitated and asked Nick something he had been churning around ever since they had met him in March. "Look," he said tentatively, "I've no idea if I'm being intrusive but I just wonder if I might have been at medical school with your parents."

Nick shot forward on his chair and stared open-mouthed at Gerry. He was speechless, completely shocked. Eventually, he found a voice, very croaky. It wasn't impossible. They would have been of an age he supposed. "I…I have, had, no idea. I…didn't know they were ever there…I…know nothing about them. My grandparents never told me anything like this. They…they lost all touch with my mother and only knew about me afterwards. Why do you think you did? Meet them, I mean."

Gerry looked long and thoughtfully at Nick. He had not expected him to know so little about his parents. He realised he had said too much. Now, wondering just how much more to say, he knew he needed to go on. "You look so like Mary I couldn't help it. I knew you had been brought up by your grandparents. We are all aware your parents had died shortly after you arrived on the scene. Putting two and two together, it seemed to add up." He shrugged his shoulders, looking very worried. By this time, Nick had lost all his colour and was shaking. He saw clearly then how big was this void in his life.

Gerry went on gently, hoping he could ease the unintended shock revelation. "They were the year below me and normally would have passed unnoticed, as students do in different years. But they became rather well known for their, um, well, wild behaviour."

"You mean they were drug addicts. Yes, I did know that much." Nick had interrupted sharply.

Gerry nodded and went on, "Your father, we understood, was the one heavily into drugs and your mother totally besotted by him. She was obviously pregnant by the time the Dean decided enough was enough and told him to leave. She was, apparently the star pupil of her first year but fell to pieces in her second. The whole affair and the fact Mother had died soon after they left, made top news in the medical school." Nick was gradually regaining some colour and composure.

After a while, he asked, "Please, did you know my father's name? I would like to find out about his family." This time Gerry firmly shook his head. He would do a little research before telling Nick the little bit he did know. Having churned it around and around since the interview in March, he did recollect the first name. Adrian. but nothing else would come. He had the inevitable mile-long medical school photograph which is taken each year somewhere at home. Unless Melanie had thrown it out during their last move. He would hunt it out and if he thought it appropriate would show Nick. Meanwhile, he needed to check whether his father could be traced, and if so if the family would want to meet him.

After a pause, Nick spoke quietly, "I wonder if my grandparents knew their daughter went to medical school. And the same one as you and me. Such a huge coincidence. I could have applied to any of them." He stopped abruptly. "Oh, how stupid of me, of course, they did. She would have gone straight from school to uni. And she was…very normal then. I now understand why Grandpa was so terribly upset when I set my heart on going to medical school, and not be part of the farm. I would have been most unwilling to take on the farm anyway. My cousin Barry was well into it by the time I finished school. He's passionate about it and it now runs so well." There was a further pause while Gerry watched the bent head, hoping to goodness no one would knock on the door. He decided the next words must come from Nick. They did. "I guess I'm going to have to tell the grandparents about this conversation. They must have approached the medical school to find out who he was and even where they went. I know Norfolk is a long way from London but I can't believe they didn't try."

Gerry nodded. "So be it, but you must realise how terribly painful this would be for them? There must be a reason why they have not told you. Are you really ready to open that particular can of worms without a lot more research of your own? For instance, where were you found? And how old were you? Do you have a valid birth certificate?"

Nick looked at Gerry, searchingly. He answered slowly, picking out each word. "Those are questions I've asked myself often but done nothing about. I've known all my adult life I could but not had the courage to explore. I hated applying for entry to medical school and applying for a passport. Silly really as I have an 'Abandoned Baby' birth certificate, which I suppose embarrasses me. Yes, I see what you mean about not telling my grandparents about our conversation." He hesitated. "I was in care all the time in Essex, so guess we all got there somehow. Perhaps that is where I should start. If I do want to know. Name change must have been done legally or it wouldn't have been on documents."

He looked up after another long pause. "Thank you. When all of this resonates, yes, I will take it further. I think it will relieve me of a lot of recurrent dreams and nightmares. That's a bit of a confession! But I will be ever more grateful to you as you have opened a whole new way of thinking."

Gerry shuffled some papers in front of him, then picking up his walking sticks, he struggled painfully into a standing position. "Go on, you get off home but drive slowly."

Nick opened the door for him, following even more slowly. Just as he reached the door into reception, Jane came through. She stopped suddenly in front of him. "For goodness sake, Nick, are you alright? You look as if you've seen a ghost."

He attempted a grin. "Perhaps I have!"

"Then go and sit in my office until you've exorcised it. I'll bring you a coffee in a few minutes," said firmly.

Gratefully, Nick did. He sank into the armchair and realised he was actually shaking. Yes, he really must face his problem, and he must do something about it. It had festered for years while he was lacking the courage to find out. Quietly, Jane returned with a steaming mug of black coffee. She'd remembered from day one just how he liked it. Nick nodded his thanks and slowly sipped it while Jane sat at her desk moving a huge pile of what looked like invoices into files. No questions asked. He looked at the ring on her finger and thought what a lovely home she must have. Gratefully, he got up and thanked her. She looked up from the pile in front of her with one finger at the place she had been reading. "Oh yes. Hope you feel better in the morning. You will be shadowing Ikbal tomorrow."

He was about to leave the premises when Penny came rushing up. "Oh, there you are!" she said hurriedly. "I thought you had gone home. Listened outside Gerry's room and it seemed totally quiet. I thought he'd be working and he's paranoid about being interrupted." She swallowed and took another breath. "But, Nick, I have four tickets for the open-air concert at Blickling on Saturday week. You've met one of the practice nurses, Liz? She thought she was going to be on her own but finds her other half is back and has already got a ticket for her. Do come with me. I don't know what sort of music you like but it's jazz and classical, I think. Suzanne and Maria are coming too. It's always such fun."

Just for a moment, Nick hesitated. Told himself not to be silly. Indeed, he had been attracted to Penny as soon as he had met her. He looked at her eager face. His heart took a couple of thuds. "Yes, yes, I'd love to come. You must tell me how when and where. Oh, and thank you for thinking of me. My social calendar is rather thin at the moment."

Feeling a little more cheerful, he was accosted yet again when he reached his car. Ikbal was waiting for him with his elbow on Nick's newly acquired three-year-old blue Ford Bmax. "Hi," he greeted Nick with a grin. "You look exhausted for such a young man."

"Young, indeed. Speak for yourself," Nick retorted, "but it has been a very concentrated day one way or another." The understatement of the year Nick thought to himself.

Ikbal turned to face him. "Just wondered if you might like to come home with me and meet Parva and my two boys tomorrow evening? It's Friday, so you can sleep in the next day. You're with me all day, so it seemed a possible idea?"

This time Nick did look happier. "I'd love too! How very kind of you. Can I bring anything?"

"Of course not," Ikbal replied, "just bring yourself." Nevertheless, he told himself, that would be one box of Thornton's chocolates, and Saturday would need another.

Chapter 3
Nick Sees Racial Abuse

He drove slowly back to the farm cottage his grandparents now occupied. The previous year they had moved out of the farmhouse into the nearby farm cottage in order for Barry to have space for his increasing family. The rest of the evening was spent telling his eager grandparents about his working day and colleagues. It cemented the idea he needed to find his own accommodation fairly quickly. The cottage, though roomy, was a great deal smaller than the farmhouse and, much as his grandparents were so happy to have him, they gave him barely enough time to think. Unwittingly their love almost overpowered him.

Friday was, if possible, even hotter. Ikbal remained in his suit looking cool, while Nick's shirt was almost sticking to him at eight in the morning. Inside it was by contrast cool. Ikbal's consulting room faced due east but horizontal blinds held the heat outside. His walls held all the usual framed certificates plus a number of photographs of his family. Nick took a careful look at Parva. She was stunningly beautiful. The boys looked about five and three years old, both sitting cross-legged on a lawn with happy smiles. Ikbal must have seen Nick's indrawn breath when he looked at the picture of

Parva. "Yes, she is beautiful. And her nature is too. Not an arranged marriage but I think an arranged marriage has something to be said for it. Parents and family do know you better than you know yourself." Nick nodded while wondering to himself how big a part a dowry or the need for a compliant wife played its part.

It was great seeing the patients through the morning. Ikbal wore his mask but made no attempt to change into scrubs as did Maria. Interesting. The patients were such a contrast from the ones at his training practice. There, in Croydon a large number, if not the majority, were from ethnic minorities. Here in Norfolk very few indeed. One or two patients recognised him from his childhood. One dear old lady forgot the urgent problem that had made the triage nurse agree to doctor consultation. She kept on and on exclaiming how wonderful it was to see Emma and Tom's little grandson grow into such a tall handsome man. And a doctor too! Ikbal could not suppress a smile, while Nick could have crawled under the carpet with embarrassment.

It was particularly useful to know which consultants the practice used for referrals. Also, good to know both he and Ikbal thought about patients in the same way. In his training practice, there had been a strict policy of 'one complaint and no more at a consultation'. Nick had hated this as he had felt so many complaints were interlinked, and how on earth did a doctor find out, admittedly on rare occasions, what was the hidden agenda? Stuck in his mind was the middle-aged lady, with almost nothing on her medical records, who came in with a sore throat but as she held the door handle to leave the room asked very diffidently if it was important to mention a lump somewhere? If Nick hadn't been staring at her as she left the room, wondering why she had really come, he was sure she would not have plucked up the courage to ask. As a result, a nice early lump in her tummy had been found and dealt with.

Between patients, Liz came in to ask if Ikbal would come and look at what looked like a nasty lump in a young lady's breast. Both he and Nick expected a cyst, so common in teenagers and young women. The patient was ready for him in Liz's consulting room. Ikbal jumped up and followed her, while Nick came slowly behind and stood in the doorway, suspecting an invasion of two men might be embarrassing.

None of them was quite prepared for the girl's reaction. She sat up, clutched the sheet to protect herself, swung her legs over the side and prepared to run. Instead of bringing her knees up, she shook all over and shouted, "Get out. Get out. I'm not 'aving one of them blacks near me." Liz held the obviously terrified girl close, while Ikbal turned and quietly left the room, nodding to Nick to take over. Liz was stroking her back telling her to quieten down and another doctor would have a look. Nick moved into a chair he had pulled up by the head of the bed and looked up. Liz stepped away indicating Nick should take the next step. The girl was struggling to get off the couch, now hampered by Nick sitting just where she would want to put her feet. She was still shaking. He asked gently, "Shall we start all over again? Please, tell me your name. I'm new here and have no idea who anyone is."

She was still shaking. "You won't let 'im near me, will you? I read all about the terrorists."

"Nick let it go, she was calming down." Liz interrupted. "Sorry, Dr Grovenor, I should have told you. This is Carol. She's actually 27 even if she does look like a teenager!" Nick nodded, still looking up at Carol. Over thin, smelling of cigarettes, confirmed by her brown stained fingers, short straight black dyed hair at all angles, black mascara now everywhere it was not meant to be, and pale blue eyes. The overall impression was of grubbiness and poverty. Probably the only relief from life was the life-threatening cigarettes. He could detect no signs of drug abuse and no smell of alcohol. He could only think how sad it was to be so ill-informed. Perhaps she didn't have a television or a smart phone. She had stopped shaking and was staring at him. He spoke, "Come on, Carol, shall we just have a look at what nurse has found? Could you bring yourself to lie back for a moment?" Liz moved into Nick's place and held Carol's hand. Very gently, he ran his hand over the lump. Not difficult to see anyway in her almost non-existent breasts. At least three centimetres across, hard and stuck to the skin. He didn't go any further with the examination. "There, that's all for now. Sit up and we'll decide what to do. Pop your clothes back on while I write something in your notes." With his back to her, it was Liz who realised she was about to make a run for it. Grabbing her by the arm, she sat her down firmly. Nick decided to take control. "Carol that lump is bad. You need to get to the hospital as soon as possible. Like today."

She almost spat at him. "Don't be so bloody silly. Who's going to pick me kid up from school? Eh? I don't let no one else pick 'er up. Too dangerous."

Slightly taken aback, Nick continued in a louder voice, "Carol, if you don't get that lump sorted, you're not going to be alive to collect your kid from school. Ever."

For the first time, the seriousness was beginning to trickle into her mind. She stared at him open mouthed. After a while, she whispered, "It ain't cancer, is it?" Nick nodded. "But it's only old people who get that! You're wrong. You've bloody well got to be."

Nick sighed. "I wish I were. Kids can get it too. You're very unlucky." Nick paused, then spoke briskly, "Now come on, is Mum or Dad anywhere near who could help? You're going to need a lot of it."

By now thoroughly alarmed, she was beginning to panic. "Me mum don't know who me dad was. She's over at Aylsham but I don't like 'er near the kid. Gives 'er sweets and biscuits and things."

Nick nodded patiently realising the wrong move could end in disaster. "Just for a while, she'll have to eat the wrong things. Well done you for knowing what to do. Wish a few other mums did. How will you get to the hospital?"

"Got me car. Ain't I?"

"Great!" said Nick with relief, not knowing what he would have done otherwise. "You go and make some arrangements with Mum and the school and I'll tell the hospital to expect you. Right?" She nodded, now in floods of tears. He left her to be looked after by Liz. On the way out, he turned, took her hand and said, "Carol, please will you come in to let me know tomorrow how it all went? And Dr Chakraborty honestly isn't a terrorist. I should know. We were at school together. I was a thin small redhead and he used to save me from the bullies. I promise you, he is the kindest person." She stared back at him not really believing.

Nick waited until Ikbal was free from his last morning patient. Nick gave him a rueful smile as he moved back to the chair he had vacated earlier. "I hope that doesn't happen too often. Shook me a bit, and goodness knows how much it must hurt you."

Ikbal shrugged. "Rarely as unreasonable and forthright as that I'm glad to say but often I get the vibes Asian doctors are not the most welcome. Can't do much about it, just try to pretend I don't notice."

"She should come and live in Croydon. In places almost only black people and just as many black doctors. She's a strange little lass, definitely a carcinoma, hopelessly uneducated and I reckon everything goes to 'the kid'. Didn't seem to have a name." Ikbal nodded. "Glad you were free. It's not easy to find that much time with one patient."

Feeling it was perhaps a slight criticism, Nick asked, "Would you really have done anything differently?"

After a moment's thought, Ikbal said, "Of course not but I would have had some concern for those still waiting."

Chapter 4
Nick and Ikbal

Nick as yet had no blood or other results to deal with so decided to go into town to do his bit of shopping. On coming out of Bonners, he almost bumped into Penny. She stepped back and asked cheerfully, "Oh, hi, how's it going? Hear you had a bit of a crisis this morning?" Nick nodded, delighted to see her. She asked, "Got time for a bite of lunch? It's my half day."

"Excellent. I'm hungry. Lead me to your waterhole." A pleasant half-hour was spent over coffee and sandwiches, and a lot of conversation.

On return to the surgery, Jane met them. She turned to Penny, "Glad to see you found him, and did you find somewhere to eat?"

"Yes, we did. Thanks for letting me know where he had gone." Nick was a little unsure whether that was a good thing or perhaps a little intrusive? However, it had been a delightful interlude.

Nick presented himself at Ikbal and Parva's home after a shower, shave, wash and change, complete with chocolates. The grandparents had been warned but when he reached the cottage to change, they were anxious to hear how his day. It all took longer than he had intended.

The modern detached house was in a cul de sac of about ten houses, each slightly different from the others. A grass border along the other side of the path around the cul de sac was newly planted with trees. The short unfenced front garden led to an attractive porch with a rather tired rose attached to one pillar. Ikbal opened the door before Nick could ring the bell, beaming a huge welcome for him to come in. The boys were dressed in pyjamas ready for bed, making him feel even more guilty for being late. He wished he had thought to bring something for them.

The delicious smell of Indian food permeated the house. Parva stepped beside Ikbal and was every bit as beautiful as the photograph, literally taking Nick's breath away. Her brilliantly coloured sari complemented her in every respect. She remained in the small entrance hall, then took the hand of the elder child and spoke in unaccented English, "This is Charles."

Charles presented his hand like a well-seasoned diplomat. "Hello," he said solemnly, "I'm Charles but I do have a proper Indian name as well." Parva laughed. "Yes, they do indeed have two names. And two languages. Both Ikbal and I went through school where the mere mention of our names caused confusion. I know times are so different now but we don't want that for them. They now have a choice. This is John. He's just three, almost out of the terrible twos but still shy and just a bit rebellious." With that, she took them off to bed leaving the men folk to drink cans of Indian beer, not Nick's favourite. Passing through the sizeable ultra-modern kitchen with a secluded dining area, then through a small utility room complete with new white washing and drying machines, they reached the outside area. The small garden had a paved terrace for a table and four chairs, a safe swing area, a large sandpit full of toys and not much else. However, the chairs were comfortable and in the slightly cooler evening, it was a joy to sit outside. His stomach was rumbling by the time the boys had settled and Parva came back, reminding him it was all his own fault for being late. Parva came out to them a little breathlessly. "Sorry it's running late. They wanted to stay down but Charles has Saturday school tomorrow and contrary to most small children, is rather fond of his bed. Heaven help us when he is a teenager! Come on through. Everything is in the hot trolley and ready to eat." It was. And what a meal of curry, cooked as Nick had never known it, so delicious and such interesting side dishes. The curried lamb was mouth-wateringly tender.

Later, after the table had been emptied of food, they took themselves and coffee outside to the comfortable chairs in the garden. "Now," said Parva firmly, "I want to hear all about your schooldays together. I've heard so many references to you, Nick but still know very little. Ikbal is very reticent on the subject."

Nick looked enquiringly at Ikbal. He looked a little rueful. "I was unsure how much you would want to pass on but I'm afraid nothing escapes Parva. She's a research biochemist and needs to know everything!"

Parva roared with laughter. "Nick, if I'm intrusive. Forgive me. I may be very insensitive but when I scent a mystery, I like to get it uncovered."

It took a little while for Nick to recover from the direct question, and decide what to say. So much of his life he had tried to obliterate. He thought perhaps this might be the moment to tell something of himself to Ikbal and Parva, knowing that was where it would stay. He took a deep breath, breaking the silence. "OK. Where to start. Both my parents, I now understand, were medical students. Mother fell for this drug addict who soon got her addicted. She left her parents, changed her name and disappeared into the drug scene. I was born, unregistered and dumped somewhere within the social services circle. Mother died shortly afterwards as I think did my father. Are you still with me?" Ikbal and Parva nodded. He went on. "I had a wonderful foster home until I was seven or so. She died of cancer; he couldn't cope and took me to Wetlands Community School near where they had picked me up as a baby from the orphanage. In reality, it was a boarding school for uncontrollable children. For years and years, I was full of bitter, festering anger at why my foster father couldn't continue looking after me. Only later, much later, did I hear he committed suicide immediately he had taken me to a place of safety." Nick stopped. The evening warmth was still there. He took another drink of his now cold coffee. The others waited until he was ready to resume. "I then spent a couple of embarrassing years being thrown out of several foster homes until in desperation social services took me back to the so-called school, now according to the placard, 'Wetlands Home for Young People'. My schooling was non-existent in those two years except for any comics I managed to steal. Most of the time playing truant if the truth is known. I had no intention of learning and goodness only knows where I would have ended, other than in prison but for my grandparents."

Here Parva interjected, "Did you get caught up in the drug scene then? You must have been a sitting duck for a supplier to use?"

"Oddly enough, I didn't," Nick replied, "I'm not even sure if the gang I went about was into drugs. Stealing was much more our line. I still shudder to remember our forays. Because of my red hair, they kept me acting as baggage man. We never went hungry. We stole food, booze, watches and gimmicks but never got caught."

Nick paused for breath. "My grandparents only knew I existed. They had never given up hope of finding me but until they employed a third professional had had no joy. He, being into all the newest technology managed to search out all the existing records and located my whereabouts. I was ten years old. An angry rebel against the whole world. Determined to have nothing to do with this new home. In the country of all places! I think if social services had had the sense to tell me they were my grandparents, it might have been easier. They had no idea how much I needed an identity. Instead, they wanted to see if it could work first; knowing how difficult I was. But my grandparents were immediately so kind and loving I couldn't stay that way. I was very small for my age, and weedy. I was hopelessly out of place at the village school at first and miles behind educationally. But I began to enjoy it. After about six months, I was catching up fast. My grandparents decided I ought to try for Postams where their daughter had been in her happy days. Knowing all the circumstances, the head decided to get an IQ test done before committing himself. Here Ikbal and I met for the first time. He spoke no, or almost no English, so was also subjected to this test."

"I never knew that!" interjected Parva.

Nick took another sip and looked at Ikbal who just nodded gently. After a while, he went on. "We must both have done pretty well. It was September and we were both admitted immediately, Ikbal as a boarder and me as a day boy. Gosh, how we both struggled in those first few weeks but it cemented a friendship we still have to this day, and will continue. I even had to learn table manners and reasonable speech. In the village school, I learnt to mind my language! I had acquired quite a strong Norfolk twang but that didn't matter as half the boys at Postams were sons of farmers. Ikbal stopped me from wanting to fight every boy who teased my skinny appearance or red hair. He even fought off some of the bullies on my behalf. Games I dreaded. I sneaked off to one of the practice rooms and found a piano. My ear was fairly good and I could pick out some tunes and put harmonies together. One day when I failed to appear at rugby, a search party was sent out to find me. I was totally absorbed when the games master himself crept into the room. Instead of the blasting I expected, he asked if I had piano lessons. Having answered negatively he then suggested I asked my grandparents to have some, and then he would excuse me from rugby. I couldn't believe my ears. As you may know, it's my major hobby now."

It was beginning to get dark so they went back inside. Nick prepared to leave, thinking he must have outstayed his welcome. "Oh, no you don't," said Parva, "I haven't finished with you yet and you've got an easy day tomorrow. Come on, there is more to say." A sweet fruit drink was put in front of him; very refreshing, probably something with mango in it.

Nick continued, "Languages were also a nightmare. The others had done a couple of years at French and Latin. Ikbal coped well with both these. They released me from Latin after a term but I had to have French before I could do A levels. I did get a C in the end. Bet you get an A, Ikbal?" Ikbal nodded. "Maths and sciences were a comparative doddle. Funnily, I loved history and English Literature. Medicine was an instinctive choice that greatly upset my grandparents. I now know why." He stopped speaking suddenly and turned to Ikbal. "Come on Ikbal, you can now fill me in with why you came to England. In all the years I've known you, you have never mentioned your parents or a thing about your life before or after Postams."

Parva got up and began to clear the table. "Nick, old chap, it's getting on for midnight. It's a very long story and just about as sad and unsettling as yours but a promise you shall hear it. I need to tell my story. I never have. Even fully to Parva. But I do have Parva." His voice had softened and he looked tenderly at her. "We met at the school in London and neither of us has ever needed more." Nick looked thoughtful, nodded, gave his thanks to Parva and left. He couldn't believe after all these years of friendship, they still knew so little about each other. He worried he might have said too much.

Chapter 5
Nick and Maria

Finding sleep difficult, partly because of the sultry heat in his small room, and partly disturbed by the memories he had uncovered that evening, Nick was further kept awake by a massive thunderstorm in the early hours. Eventually drifting off into a restless sleep, he was awakened by his grandmother banging on the door. "Nick, are you all right? You're going to be late if you don't hurry. Breakfast is all ready for you. Said you're to be at that place in Cromer by 10." It was lovely to be spoilt like this but he must take control of his own life. Job for the day was, once he'd seen the doctor in Cromer who was to show him how the cooperative worked, he would be scheduled to do some shifts covering out of hours services. Not too arduous. It was midday before he returned to Mersham. It was crowded with tourists and so hot. A few perfunctory visits to estate agents to register his need for a flat was as far as he got.

Monday morning, Maria was waiting for him with the inevitable cup of coffee in her hand. "Come on, Nick. You're with me. We're on emergencies and same day problems. I'll be changing into scrubs later as I feel more comfortable. Got a mask? Some patients like us to use one; got used to it during the worst of Covid-19. If that's ever going to be over. Now, first visit is a request from a midwife. Baby arrived at home in such a hurry that Mum couldn't get to hospital. Happens here. 30 odd miles and bloody awful traffic in places. Midwife says the older sibling not her department but she's worried. Thinks the baby's sister has got a funny eye. My guess is it's got epicanthic folds. Always makes them look like they're squinting or oriental. Single mum, another yet older kid and no car. Partner possibly coming back. As ever." Maria drove rather as she spoke. Rather jerkily. Nick was not entirely happy as it had started to pour with rain and he could barely see through the windscreen of her very ancient Saab. They arrived at a row of terraced cottages with doors opening directly into a busy road. Inevitably, there was a row of cars tightly packed, half on pavements in a seemingly never-ending stream. Eventually, they found a space some way from their destination. Maria had a long waterproof cagoule but Nick just had to make a dash for it, having forgotten as usual to bring anything waterproof.

Maria flung open the door without knocking, shouting as she did so. "Hello! Dr Skowron here. Where are you?"

A tall thin middle-aged woman with greying hair, large dark glasses and a worn-looking flower print dress came in from the back room smoking a cigarette, glaring at them. "Jan goes upstairs as she doesn't like me smoking near the baby. I got the other two out in the garden, in the rain, I might add. I'll bring Lisa up when I can get her out of the mud."

Maria humped past her. "Shouldn't be smoking near the other two either. You her mum? You'd better bring the little one upstairs." Puffing, she climbed the steep stairs which ran straight out of the front room. The woman nodded, turned and slammed the door behind her.

Mum, in her nightgown was leaning back against the cushions cradling the baby on her lap. She grinned at Maria. "Heard you had a run-in with my mum. I've given up."

Maria grinned back at her. "When did this arrive? Looks new."

Jan laughed. "It's yet another girl. Had lots of boys' names but ever since I've known it was a girl, my mind is a blank. Yesterday evening. Can't see anything wrong with Lisa's eye so guess you're wasting your time but hey ho, if whatever the midwife's name is thinks there's something wrong, there must be a fuss."

Neither Nick nor Maria heard Grandmother come up the stairs dragging a soaking wet Lisa behind her. Maria asked conversationally, well knowing the answer, "Where's your other half then?"

A huge snort from behind. "Him? He buggers off as soon as he can't get his oats."

"Mum! Lay off! He's not that bad. Don't go on. Not in front of the kids."

"Never could stand him. Likes the pub better than you. Lazy sod, doesn't do a day's work if he has enough pocket money for his pint." Jan now sitting up in bed disturbed the baby who started howling as Jan tried to stop the flow of invective.

"Mum, go away! And let the doctor get on." With that, Maria's mobile rang. She hauled herself out of the chair to distance herself from the noise. A few seconds later, she came back. "Nick, please would you see if you can find anything amiss with the nameless baby's sister? One of my brats has been sick over the floor at school. Told me she felt sick. Didn't believe her. Could be half an hour. Her dad's at home so he can see to her when she's cleaned up." Nick sat down in the chair Maria had just vacated, reached out and took the crying baby away from Jan. A wave of emotion flooded him. He wanted a wife and he wanted a baby. It was so intense he tried to imagine it was real. The baby stopped crying and looked up at him. He tried to make Penny fit the place where he wanted a wife but someone else he couldn't place was there already. He handed the baby back letting Jan pop the not too clean dummy back in her mouth. Encouraged by Jan, Lisa crossed in front of Nick to sit with her mother. She stared at Nick with wide-open bluest of eyes and he saw clearly what the midwife had seen; clever woman for spotting it. Even cleverer for knowing it could be serious. A white mark deep inside the eye. Hopefully not but probably a vain hope. A malignant cancer called retinoblastoma is poor news at any age. Between one and two years was the most common age as far as he could remember. Terribly rare. However, he was in no doubt the baby needed to be seen soonest possible. "How old is Lisa? Nick enquired quietly.

"Just 13 months. Never thought I'd fall as quickly as this. I'll know better this time." She was a chubby pretty little girl with her fair curly head of hair plastered in muddy sand.

"Yep. Better make sure. You don't need another one that quickly again. Get yourself an appointment with family planning and carry it through! Now, this young lady here" – Nick gently tapped Lisa's knee – "needs to be seen at the eye unit at the N and N and in the next few days. Sometimes that white dot in her eye can be very serious. Other times, it's not. Had you noticed it?"

"Yea, saw it a few weeks ago and didn't think anything of it. Now you say it, it does look bigger today. How bad?"

"The very worst is she may lose the eye if you don't get it seen soon."

Jan suddenly looked near tears but just rocked the baby and hugged Lisa. "How on earth can I get her there? Neither my mum nor I drive." Nick thought her tough, instead of throwing a fit of hysterics, she went straight for the practical problem.

He got up. "We'll work that one out. I'm new, so will need to organise a little. Are you breastfeeding?"

"O God, no. Haven't time to faff around with that. Tried with number one but never again." With that, Nick's phone rang. Jane was outside whenever he was ready.

She leant across the passenger seat opening the door of her ancient Ka to let Nick in. As she fixed her seat belt, she asked, "Problems?"

"Yep," Nick replied. "After less than two weeks here, I've seen more serious things than I can remember in months at my training practice. Can't believe it. I'm more than a little concerned. How kind of you to come and find me. I was about to ring for a lift."

Jane grinned. "Maria rang to ask calls should be diverted to you as she had to collect Sophia from school. I guessed she might even have forgotten she had deserted you. Checked visiting list. Oh, and by the way, there's a young lady insisting you told her to come in. She's not been there long but agitated in a big way."

Nick shook his head, and then remembered. "Of course, I saw her yesterday and really do want to know how she got on. Now I need to sort this little girl out too."

"Could I help?" asked Jane quietly.

"Yes, yes," he answered eagerly, "I'd be so grateful if you could. I really don't quite know how to arrange transport or an urgent paediatric eye clinic appointment. Makes me feel like a fish out of water."

This time Jane laughed. "Nick, you'll have to realise this is not Jordon. You do not have to do everything. We do have a great band of volunteer drivers. And, some of us know our way around urgent appointments! However, I do need a diagnosis and a few facts." Gratefully, Nick briefly related the essential facts, exited the car and made for his room and Carol. Jane followed him with her eyes. He was going to be such an asset to the practice. She quashed the comfortable feeling she had had with the brief time they had spent in the car.

Nick collected Carol on his way through the waiting area, and still rather breathless, apologised for being late. "Cor," came the reply, "never heard one of you lot say sorry before!"

Nick decided she did have a sense of fun, despite her troubles. He replied wryly, "Just I hate hanging around waiting, and guess you do too. Now, you seem to have survived yesterday. Tell me about it."

"Well, had to make it up with me mum first. Didn't tell you but we'd fallen out. Big time. Realised what you'd been saying on the way over. Told me mum. Told me I was a bloody fool the way I lived. Any road, she's happy to have the kid and the kid is happy. Left her to sleep over. Once I got there and me ticker stopped chasing and I found where to go, everyone was real nice. The doctor was an old lady and said what you said. I'm starting with radio something on Monday. Then I have to go for jabs and much later, they'll take it out.

I've got it all written down and a phone number to ring, any time I get scared or want to talk. And I don't have to drive there. They send someone."

Nick looked at her, delighted. "Carol you're wonderful. Difficult to remember it was you yesterday." This time the tears began to come. No mascara today. He handed her a handful of tissues from his desk.

"Yeh, well," she spoke between sobs, "I've got the kid, haven't I? And I don't want to die just yet." Nick quietly reflected she might well not see 'the kid' grow up but advances now with immunotherapy and many other avenues, might well prolong her life for a very long time.

Chapter 6
Nick and Penny

The rest of the weeks passed quickly, if in a bit of a haze, with so many different things to learn and understand. His time with Penny he found interesting. She was so relaxed with online and telephone consultations. She had a prodigious memory for family details and always spent some time just chatting. Nick liked that. It made patients comfortable and able to talk. Only two patients came in for the face to face consultations. She greeted them like friends and they responded in the same way. One very elderly lady even was able to giggle and tell her she hadn't been called Maud, ever. Might be on her records but she was Rose to everyone. Penny looked devastated. "I'm so sorry. Trouble is with you seniors the information on your wartime identity cards was the one used on the old Lloyd George envelopes. They're still around, you know those buff things that used to hold all your records?" Rose nodded. "And they were taken from birth registrations. Blame your parents. Rose it shall be." Now thoroughly relaxed, Rose was able to describe her 'down below' problems. Nick waited outside.

Despite another thunderstorm in the night, Saturday dawned bright and sunny. He hoped it would last until evening as he did not feel like sitting under an umbrella to watch a concert, especially now the temperature was dropping back to a more normal range. The morning he was determined to devote his time to finding a flat in which to be independent. And some pictures with which to decorate his consulting room; not for his family photos or even the awful one of him in his graduation gown.

One bit of Nick was really looking forward to the evening. He loved music in almost any form, jazz being one of his least favourites. However, it was a very long time since he had had an entertainment to attend. The other and larger bit of him almost dreaded social occasions. He knew he got tongue-tied in a group, never thinking of the right responses, nor could he think of what to say. At school, he was secure whilst Ikbal was there, utterly bereft when he left so suddenly. He became known as a loner who liked his piano better than his peers. University had been much better. They were all busy with one great interest in all things medical. He joined the choral society, table tennis and various other clubs but again they were organised, not social occasions. The girls made a beeline for him, and he tried to respond. A couple of girls he did become very friendly with but folded up completely when it got as far as bed. Much of it, he knew was due to his early upbringing. He still had terrible flashbacks and nightmares. One day, he would get help but he was always pushing the thought to the back of his mind. He did at one stage wonder if he could be gay but hard as he tried to grasp the idea, he knew he was definitely heterosexual. He was over 30 and had never had a serious relationship, much as he would have loved one. The shock he had had on picking up the baby, the intense longing for a family, he could only compare with the moment he discovered he might have grandparents and so he actually belonged to someone.

Another problem was wine. He had eventually promised to bring a couple of bottles as well as the chocolates that evening as his contribution. He enjoyed a glass of beer or wine but had never found pub gatherings or parties particularly enjoyable. Probably inherited that from his teetotal grandparents. However, the wine merchant was more than helpful, without discovering how little Nick knew about the subject. Nick had also offered himself as driver knowing this would give him every excuse to drink little or nothing.

The flat searching was less successful. He was now signed on with the three estate agents. The flats available were either far too large or unsuitable. One agent thought he might have a good one in a few weeks when the tourists had gone home. More likely he was waiting for some holidaymaker with a long term let to cancel. But he did find two beautiful Norfolk landscapes for his consulting room.

Later, dressed in casual khaki slacks with a bright blue short-sleeved shirt, and a warm fawn cashmere pullover at the ready should the evening chill, Nick set off to pick up Suzanne and Maria to meet at Penny's flat for a pre-concert drink. Suzanne texted to say she was running late and would pick up Maria and meet him at Penny's.

Penny's address was in a very upmarket part of Mersham. Nick began to wonder if he actually had the right address. The forecourt was impeccably manicured with a small lawned roundabout and immaculate beds of huge flowers at each side. He stopped in front of an oak front door with polished brass fittings glowing in the sun. Two cars were parked further around; a Porsche and a newish looking Mini. There seemed to be only one bell. Rather diffidently, Nick rang it wondering again if he had the right address. This looked like a very, very elegant house with its three-storied, ivy-clad walls, latticed windows and perfect garden. Not flats.

The door opened suddenly and a breathless Penny stood back to let Nick in. "Oh, Nick. So glad you could get here for an early drink before we head off for Blickling. The traffic is always horrendous. My flat is on third floor." Rapidly Penny took the stairs two at a time. Nick followed a bit more sedately. There were six other people in the room all holding glasses of wine. And what a room! Large and airy with two tall windows looking onto the road in front. The sun was shining straight into the room itself; two double settees, three armchairs all upholstered in a light green sitting on a massive Chinese carpet with the same shade of green as a background. Occasional tables were scattered around the room with a corner cupboard open, displaying a large variety of drinks. Nick took a deep breath. This was not what he had expected. Nor the group of people chattering loudly holding full glasses. Exactly the situation he dreaded. They all stopped chatting and turned to look at him. With a forced smile, he greeted them with a cheerful sounding "Hi". Penny made rapid introductions rendering Nick speechless. The conversation resumed as if he were not there. Oh, when would Suzanne come? At least he knew her and Maria. He rarely ran into Suzanne during working hours. Part-time work, he knew, often involved missing coffee and lunch breaks to keep up with the backlog.

Then one very elegant lady dressed entirely in a long flowing black evening dress with long dangling earrings, also black, turned to him and asked, "Are you with us tomorrow? Gorgeous!"

"Where, what and when are we talking about?" asked Nick, trying to sound interested. He disliked intensely being called 'Gorgeous'. Made him squirm.

"The rally, of course!" She raised her voice and shouted to Penny who was trying to find Nick a soft drink. "Hey, Pen, you haven't enrolled gorgeous here in the rally. You must!" Still totally bemused, he looked from one to the other hoping one of them would enlighten him.

Penny apologised, "Sorry Nick, I'm not surprised we're all talking gibberish. We're all travelling to London tomorrow to join the BAME, you know, the Black, Asia and Ethnic Minority rally. We're all passionate about it." Whatever Nick had expected from Penny, it was not that. Her enthusiasm was evident. In these plush surroundings, it sounded almost bizarre. She continued, waving her hand at him. "I'll fill you in later but we still have Suzanne and Maria to join within the carpark in three-quarters of an hour. Suzanne's Amazon delivery was late so they couldn't join us here." Nick guessed they knew a thing or two and used it as a convenient excuse. She raised her voice to be heard above the hubbub, "Drink up all, we must go in ten minutes." Two of them rushed over to fill their glasses before moving off. Nick was more than a little surprised any one of the six should be driving. They looked well-oiled already. He had told a rather surprised Penny that he would have one drink and one drink only during the evening if he were the driver. Rather dismissively, she had replied, "O, come on, Nick, this is the country. The odds of being caught are zero. I've never seen any police car or trap on the roads we travel. If I've had a couple too many, I just avoid all the main roads." Nick had shrugged. A crash, whether her fault or not her fault would mean a loss of licence. He had let it go.

Suzanne and Maria were ready and waiting by the time he and Penny arrived. Nick had found it an interesting drive. Shortly after reaching the windy tree-lined road to Aylsham, they had fallen into a very long slow queue of cars, all apparently with the same destination in view; passed one exit from the park, and then turning left just before the house itself. Nick had only moments to glance at the magnificent house itself. The Buckinghamshire Arms was full of diners and drinkers both inside and out flowing onto the narrow, temporarily one-way road leading to the park entrance. It was a glorious evening. The car parking on dry grass was well directed and easy. He had heard in very wet weather it was possible to get bogged down and need towing out by tractors. Between them, they managed to carry rugs, food and drink up to the sloping grass. They had a wonderful view looking down on the orchestra. A couple of the musicians were beginning to tune up. Everywhere was chatter and excitement. With nearly an hour before the performance started, it was decided to tuck in and eat.

"How did the flat hunting go, Nick?" asked Suzanne undoing a large bag of crisps.

With his one glass of white wine in his hand, he answered her enquiry. "No, not much luck. Flats seem hard to come by here. Had the chance of three viewings but none of them made sense. Second homeowners and long-term holidaymakers are the problem. I gather they account for the shortage. Told to try again next week."

Penny interrupted excitedly, "I didn't know you were flat hunting, Nick, I thought you were happy living with your grandparents. In fact, I thought they needed you?"

Nick hesitated for a moment. "You're right on both counts," he replied slowly, "I love being with them but they almost stifle me with their wonderful love. As yet they are both independent and were actually managing perfectly well with no help before I appeared on the scene. Just, they are both over 80, and well, I owe them everything. Need to be near when needed." He shrugged his shoulders. No one could understand what he owed them.

"Oh, if that's it!" exclaimed Penny. "I've got a spare bedroom with en-suite shower and small sitting room. As you've seen there's plenty of room in the flat."

There was a loud exclamation from Suzanne. "Don't you dare!" She spoke before Penny could say more. "Nick! Tongues wag in a small community and the smallest hint you've popped into bed with Penny before you've been here for five minutes would be the gossip of the town."

Nick turned a brilliant red. Feeling very embarrassed and socially inept he attempted a laugh. "Wouldn't be able to afford a flat-share like that anyway."

Penny hastily swallowed the piece of egg sandwich she was eating. "Nick, you don't think I rent that flat, do you? The house belongs to my diplomat parents who use it as a base when, and I mean when, in the UK. They tipped me upstairs years ago when my loud music started to drive them barmy."

"Oh," replied Nick nodding his head. "Now I do understand. I could not see how any GP could afford anything like that!"

"It's over-furnished with furniture no longer needed in the main part of the house. The parents have a habit of bringing back lovely things they find overseas." This time it was Penny who looked slightly embarrassed. "I hate having all that stuff around me!" She said vehemently. "That's why I joined the Labour Party!"

Maria groaned. "Come on, Penny, leave it be for now. Nick's here to enjoy an evening out. Not listen to the next Manifesto."

Penny laughed. "Touché."

The first half of the concert was a wonderful Classical Jazz group. Even Nick, who claimed not to be a fan, recognised pieces by Bernstein and Copland, thoroughly enjoying them as well as trying to get to grips with much he did not recognise.

The sun was just beginning to go down during the interval when a balloon flew slowly across the arena. The waves of cheers made everyone look up and join in. The passengers in the balloon were having a wonderful time gazing down on them all. Striped in white and blue with the large basket made of wicker there were at least four occupants. Closely behind followed another five balloons at different heights and distances. Brightly coloured and bringing a sense of occasion, increasing Nick's pleasure in the evening. Suzanne and Maria had disappeared when they looked down again. "Guess they've found someone they know or else gone to find a loo," suggested Penny. She moved a little closer to Nick just brushing his thigh. A frisson of excitement made him feel uncomfortable and move a fraction away.

"Now we've got a minute," Nick asked, "what is this rally you're going to tomorrow? They didn't exactly look like Labour Party friends."

Penny stood up. "Come on, let's stretch our legs before I get stuck in this position. Usually bring chairs, not just rugs. We've got a short while now we've finished off all the food. Gosh, that raspberry dish Suzanne made was scrummy."

Nick unfolded his long legs and gratefully stretched. "Yes, you're right. Now, please tell me what it's all about."

"Well, um, where to start? It's some of the BAME group plus some of the Extinction and Me2 ones who are joining us. It's probably not obvious but I do have a serious side. I'm passionate about equality, particularly of race. It all started when I saw the way one or two patients treated Ikbal. You couldn't have a nicer or gentler person. There aren't many black people here but it's no excuse. And I feel it's up to people how they feel if they are homosexual. Does it really matter if they are happy? And why should they be condemned to a life of loneliness just because some purists thinks it wrong? I could go on forever. Transgender doesn't worry me either, and I'm beginning to understand it. Sorry, Nick, I really can go on forever once started." Sounding more and more enthusiastic, Penny stopped to draw breath. Turning to look at Nick to see how he was taking it, she smiled tentatively.

"Yes," Nick said slowly, looking straight in front. "Yes, yes I can see. I had a horrid experience of seeing racial prejudice. Ikbal just took it. Do you really think rallies have any effect other than to alienate the public?"

"Yes!" she said vehemently. "Just look at the anti-slavery effort in 2019. It took down statues and almost all institutions.

However, I don't agree with going back on history. You can't change it. It's the future that matters but it did work."

The orchestra was beginning to tune up, this time a programme of traditional classical music. "One last question," Nick said quickly. "Why the expensive friends?"

"Easy," she replied. "Cash. Coaches are expensive. They think it's a great day out and can fund a coach without thinking of it more than pocket money."

Twice in the car on the way back to Penny's abode, she deliberately touched him, on the arm only but he had no doubt what she meant. The invitation to have a final drink in her flat confirmed it. He was not ready for that yet. Knowing most men would have jumped at the opportunity, yet again he knew he had problems to sort.

Nick lay in bed that night having had a wonderful evening. And full of approval for Penny's willingness to do something, rather than talking. For once, there were no nightmares.

Chapter 7
Nick Finds a Flat

"Nick, Nick have you time…" Penny spoke loudly as she stood by the stairs and saw Nick's door open. Jane had been just outside his consulting room waiting for him to finish his last consultation and held a hand up to Penny.

"Just a moment, please." She turned to face Nick. "Do I understand you are looking for a flat?"

Nick swivelled around to face her. "Too right, I am!"

Jane continued, "I met a friend this morning and he said you had been into his office to put your name down for one. Do you remember the funeral director who used to have a frontage at the far end of the high street? It's been empty for ages." Nick shook his head. "Well, this morning he was approached by a florist who wanted the shop area but not the flat but would only buy it if the right sort of person took the flat. Tim told her he knew a nice young chappie; his words, not mine. He'd like a decision asap, so I have the key if you'd like to take a little walk if you've finished for the morning."

Penny had joined them. "Or, I could take him if you're busy, Jane. I know exactly where you mean."

Jane spoke quietly but determinably. "No, that's fine, Penny but I've promised not to let go of the one and only key.

But thanks, that was a kind thought." In a way, he was grateful to Jane. He wanted to make up his own mind, not have the place furnished before he could take a proper look.

They walked companionly the few hundred yards to the empty premises. The outside was not prepossessing, being badly in need of more than a coat of paint to change the funereal exterior into a florist shop. It stood back about ten yards from the actual road, with cobbled paving in front. Jane unlocked the front glazed door still embossed with 'Funeral Services'. His entrance would be through the shop by a door faintly labelled 'Private'. He guessed the florist lady would be mostly using the double swing doors for her business. The uncarpeted stairs were basic but the room into which they opened was a pleasant surprise; sizeable and sunny. It must extend over the whole of the original funeral premises. Two large sash windows looked over the high street. Nick pulled a face as he tried unsuccessfully to open one of them, ending up covered in spider's webs and dust. A door at the far end opened into a kitchen of sorts. A blackened cooker, a filthy butler's pantry sink and a slimy wooden draining board. Not much space for a serious cook. The floor in the living room was at least bare boards but the sooner the linoleum in the kitchen was removed, the better the place would smell. The bedroom at the back would just about take a wardrobe, chest of drawers and at a pinch, a double bed. With his long legs, he needed it to be double. The primitive bathroom and loo led from the bedroom. Nick trusted there were downstairs facilities too. That point he would need to check. He hadn't realised until he looked out of the back window how much of a corner building it was. The tall trees which lined the side street almost touched the window.

For some inexplicable reason, he felt at home in it. He knew the sunshine was deceptive. There would need to be many discussions about who was responsible for what. His instinct was to start scrubbing and decorating the place. All the time Nick had been taking it in, Jane had steadily watched him, almost knowing what he was thinking. As Nick took one last look from the front window, Jane quietly asked, "Well, verdict?"

"I'm going to take it. Goodness knows why. It needs total restoration and I guess I'll be doing some of it."

Jane nodded approval. "Somehow, I thought you would. Tim was a great friend of my husband's and one of the few people who knows what happened." She stopped suddenly. She spoke as if to herself while shaking her head. "Why on earth did I say that. It just came out. Sorry. To go back to the flat. I believe the florist is happy just to let you have it and occupy the premises, if and this is the big if, you'll do your own interior decorating and furnishing."

Nick smiled. "Perfect. I'd love to. My grandparents have a barn full of excess stuff from the big farmhouse when they moved to the farm cottage, and I think they only kept it against the day when I might need it. And, I think Gramps would love to get his hand in to help. He is badly in need of occupation. One of the reasons they're trying to keep me at home."

As they walked back to the surgery, Nick wondered how different it would have been if Penny, and not Jane had been with him. Jane was so peaceful and gave him time to think. And what had she meant by that odd reference to her husband?

Fortunately, he had brought sandwiches for lunch or rather Grandmother had packed some for him. He had barely time to swallow one and carry a cup of coffee to his room before his first telephone consultation came in. For a first proper working day, it was very busy and eventful. Mondays always were anyway.

Emma had his meal on the table as usual. Tom joined them and enquired how the day had been. Nick swallowed hard. "It's a good place to be. It really is." He swallowed hard again. "I found a flat today." He watched their faces fall. "But I think I've gone crazy and will need a lot of help; flats aren't easy to find in Mershams; they get bought up by the tourist industry. I really would like to be nearer the surgery and perhaps be flexible in the evenings. I'm looking into a choir to join." He took another couple of mouthfuls of the delicious beef casserole. "It's over the old funeral place at the end of the high street. Know it?" Both nodded. "It's in a terrible state of disrepair and will take a lot done before I can move in. Do you know of a good decorator who could cope with it?"

Tom's face lit up. "I do! Me! I restored this cottage from almost falling down. A flat sound like a doddle." Nick gave a huge sigh of relief. That was the response he had hoped for.

Emma chimed in, "Will you be able to use some of the stuff in the barn? There are some lovely carpets and a lot of long curtains? I can shorten them if you like."

Nick had another night free from nightmares. He must find an opportunity to discover Jane's past. He felt so comfortable with her.

Chapter 8
Nick Meets Yuri

Autumn was definitely coming. The silver birch opposite the surgery had a number of yellowing leaves and there was a distinct feel of chill in the wind. The flat was a success. Not fully decorated yet but he had happily settled in amidst the paint and paraphernalia.

He walked in from the surgery car park with Liz, the practice nurse. A very efficient lady he had discovered. She'd just succeeded in making the jump from practice nurse to nurse practitioner after five years of extra study. To make easy conversation, he asked her how she had enjoyed the concert at Blickling. "I didn't get there. You had my ticket," was the terse reply.

Nick felt most uncomfortable. "I was told your husband had already got a ticket for you and this was a spare."

"Well," she said, still in a hard voice, "you shouldn't believe everything you are told." She strode off leaving Nick thoroughly discomfited. Perhaps he should take Penny to the task? Maybe not. It could have just been a misunderstanding.

Nick was beginning to notice a slight coolness whenever he mentioned Penny; more noticeable in the last few weeks as he had been seen around with her a fair amount. At some stage, he would need to have a real conversation with her. He was very attracted to her, of that he had no doubt but there was also a part of her he did not understand. She had obviously become infatuated with him and wanted to take things further. Time and time again she managed to touch him, sometimes so suggestively he had difficulty in coping with it. In no way was he ready to get into bed with her. All the right hormones were circulating, the desire was there but he knew only too well nothing would come of it. He had tried before and failed at the last moment. So utterly humiliating. There was a big gremlin stopping him. It was getting more and more difficult now he had moved into his flat. On one occasion, she had appeared on his doorstep at 11 at night saying she'd lost her house keys. He had found them in her bag and sent her packing.

Nick knew yet again, sorting himself out was becoming a priority task, if he and Penny were to have any future plans. Every time a relationship started getting close, he knew he clammed up. The gremlins of his childhood recurred. No one was going to find a counsellor or psychologist for him unless he asked. There was plenty of help available, and he should, more than most people, know where to look.

Maria greeted him as he walked through the door. "Hey, what's up with you? You look a bit down. Practice not up to your hopes then?"

Nick shook his head and gave her a smile. "Golly, no. It's better than I'd dreamed it could be. No just had a bit of a surprise I didn't like."

Maria decided this was not the time for questions. "OK. Well, I reckon you need a change from cooking your own meals. I can manage a couple of proper home-cooked ones too. Suggest you come back with me tonight, meet my husband, Yuri, and the girls and get stuffed with food. You're too skinny." Nick opened his mouth to come back with some rude remark about her weight but thought better of it. Maria gave a girlish giggle. "I know exactly what you're thinking and I always tell my patients not to do as I do but to eat properly. I just enjoy food. I enjoy cooking it. And I enjoy eating it. I'm a good baker too. You must try some of my cakes, they're good."

"I'd love to," Nick replied happily. He liked Maria and her home sounded fun.

Maria went to move off. "See you at about seven. Don't you dare bring anything. It's a ghastly habit some people have."

Obeying instructions as far as the adults went, Nick had no compunction about buying a novelty set of coloured pencils in very pretty upright boxes for the girls. Rather as he had expected, Maria and her family lived well outside the town in an isolated white-washed converted barn. It suited her character so well. The front garden was slightly overgrown but a goodly supply of sprouts, broccoli and cabbages were winning the fight for existence. Scattered everywhere on paths, gardens and vegetable patches were bright orange old-fashioned marigolds. The door was wide open even before Nick had parked his car. An elderly retriever wandered down the path to meet him. Two giggling little girls were jumping up and down watching his progress. Clutching his gifts, he stood just in front of them waiting for a chance to get past. He looked down. The older one couldn't stand still. "I know who you are," she said pointing somewhere in the middle of his stomach. "You're Nick. You don't know who I am, do you?"

He kept a straight face. "You are…Winnie the Pooh?" With that, she became hysterical with laughter.

Maria appeared at that moment and took a hand from each. "How rude! This one" – she pulled the right hand one forward – "is Tanya, and this other one who seems to have no manners is Sophia. At eight years of age, I would expect better."

The smaller one decided to be involved. "And I'm Tanya and I'm six. At least I was last week." Nick handed each girl who, whatever Maria had said, that which seemed to expected of him. After a hasty thank you, they fled to the room behind. Nick looked up at the rafters high above the entrance cum dining room. Glass had been let into part of the roof making the room full of the evening sunlight. A broad staircase led up to a balcony on three sides, presumably where the bedrooms were. He followed Maria through to their living/sitting room/lounge or whatever they called it. So exactly like the old farmhouse where he had spent his teenage years. And in just the homely mess and muddle which made it a home. Full-length narrow windows looked out to a lake beyond their fence. The lawn, or pretentions to one, at the back, held a couple of swings and a massive homemade climbing frame.

"I'm glad, Nikolaus, you like my view." Nick turned to see where the heavily accented voice came from. To his surprise, he saw a small man in a wheelchair. He presumed this was Yuri. He tried to place the nationality. Polish, he guessed. But it didn't sound like a Polish name. Rightly assuming, Maria had not thought to tell Nick about him. Yuri added, "I am Polish, Nikolaus, they call me Yuri. Not my name but I am used to it." Maria had retreated to the kitchen, shouting at the girls to wash their hands ready for tea leaving him alone. Yuri looked older than Maria and was obviously very disabled. He had the most piercing eyes Nick had come across, a balding head and an infectious smile. "You see, Nikolaus, I have the multiple sclerosis which is not good. The immunotherapy I think help. But I must do other things I can do. I like the birds. I like to look and see if one I do not know comes to the water."

Nick studied him for a few moments. "And what else do you do? I can't see you watching birds all day."

"Have they not told you, Nikolaus? I can no longer be an architect, so I give up and now I search for people who are missing or who might or might not be dead. Nick opened his mouth to speak but at that moment, they were also called in for tea. Tea was the main meal of the day in Norfolk.

The kitchen was a large square room, with a low ceiling. A red AGA was giving its gentle warmth, the dog stretched out in front of it, the whole place was Nick's idea of a perfect kitchen. "Nikolaus," said Yuri, "I can read your mind. You think the AGA is not eco. It pumps out the unwanted heat. It burn oil? It does. But it is a home for me."

"You're so wrong," retorted Nick. "I'd never employ you as a mind reader. I was thinking how absolutely perfect this kitchen is, and how, one day, I would like one just like it." Yuri laughed. His speech was slightly slurred as was his laugh. Maria beamed as she served out huge platefuls of delicious smelling chicken casserole. For the next half hour, the children took over the conversation as they ploughed through their meal telling them all about school and what they hoped Father Christmas might be persuaded to bring. Nick had eaten so well he barely had room for the outstanding ginger pudding. Maria was right, she could cook. And she could eat.

The children having been told they could have half an hour on their tablets, and then it was shower and bed, retreated to the little back snug. Maria refused offers of help to clear but left Yuri and Nick to chat. They moved to the conservatory to see the last of the sunset over the lake. "So, you like my kitchen, Nikolaus. One day I design a house for you. In my mind but you can draw it."

"Yuri," began Nick diffidently, "may I change the subject just for a moment? I need some research done for myself and, from what you indicated, I wonder if you could have a go at finding my father's family? I've got a little way along the line but really have no idea how I should progress. And, if you do undertake it, it must be at the going rate."

Yuri surveyed him for some time. "Yes, Nikolaus. I will try to find your father."

Nick shook his head. "No, no he is long dead," he interrupted, "soon after I was born. So is my mother. My wonderful grandparents used a researcher and after 12 years found me. I...I just would like to know if I have other grandparents."

"I see." Nodded Yuri. Nick spent the next ten minutes giving Yuri as full a background as he could. Neither of them had noticed Maria creep in.

"Do you know Nick?" she said quietly when he had finished. "I didn't have any idea you carried so much baggage around. You're amazing. How does it affect you? It absolutely must."

Having told Yuri so much of his life, it was difficult not to continue. "In a lot of ways, I suppose. My grandparents are the best in the world but old fashioned even for their era. I am paralysed on social occasions. I find getting close to people difficult, I have nightmares. Enough?"

Maria hesitated. "I doubt that's even the least of your baggage. I thought you were getting close to Penny?"

This time it was Nick who hesitated. "Not that sort of close. She likes an escort and some of the time I can go along with it. I cannot take her friends or causes."

"OK!" said Maria decisively. "She was seen going into your flat at 11 pm one evening. That doesn't leave much room for any other interpretation."

"Well, it does," Nick sounded angry and upset. "She appeared at my door saying she had lost her keys and would I take her home to get replacements. I tipped her somewhat copious handbag upside down and there they were. No, she is not getting into bed with me if that is the rumour."

"It is, and it's not doing you much good. I'll do my best to quash it. And I'm so relieved. I had thought better of you. She is very good at hooking men." Nick relaxed enough to pick up and drink the nearly cold cup of coffee in front of him.

Yuri broke the silence. "Nikolaus, I get tired quickly and it takes time to get to bed. I wish you a good night." Nick stood up and walked to the door with him, then returned to his armchair.

"Does anyone else know about your background?" asked Maria.

Nick thought for a moment and decided to tell her as much as he could. "Charles knows most of it and Ikbal knows how utterly raw and out of place I was at school. The whole story is too long and too complicated, foster homes, ended up in a…it needs a book to write it all down. But for my grandparents, I would have ended up in prison most of my life." Nick, whose gaze at been fixed on the coffee cup looked up to see how Maria was taking it. She was looking at him thoughtfully.

"No wonder you are so good with children and patients. They don't need socialising. Have you ever thought of professional help?"

Nick nodded. "Many times, but I just don't feel ready to do it."

"When you do, let me know. I really do know someone good."

By way of changing the subject, Nick enquired, "How long has Yuri had MS?"

"About five years, since we noticed he was walking badly. He has gone downhill quite steadily and not really halted by the immunotherapy. He was never as tall as me but he seems to have shrunk and there is less and less he can do around the house. We've had a lift installed which quite surprisingly works after the number of times the kids have gone up and down in it. Charles has been a huge support but the staff and other doctors have no idea how ill he really is. I'm afraid it's why I'm often a bit late if he needs extra help in the mornings. I try to make a joke of it."

Nick got up, gave a pat to the dog who had been sitting on his feet. "Maria, it's time I went. Thank you for a wonderful meal. I would feel very privileged to help out in any way I can. As you say, children, I can enjoy. Your two are a delight. I can have them for a Saturday or babysit, collect them from school or whatever is helpful. Just let me know."

Chapter 9
A Romantic Meal

Penny was keen to view the flat. Nick was unwilling, partly because it was a work in progress but mostly because he did not want to be alone with her in the flat. He prevaricated, trying to find a solution. So far, attracted as he was, there were too many reservations for him to want intimacy. He decided it was time he took her out for a meal instead. Then they could visit the new flat very briefly on the way. Graftons was a local expensive and reputedly good restaurant.

After his visit to Maria, he realised how careful he would need to be.

Nick was looking his best in his dark suit, even wearing his medical school tie. Penny looked stunning in her red mid-calf dress which clung to her, just flaring at the hem. Her cleavage was, as she intended, very provocative. They made a very handsome couple. He left the downstairs doors open and the lights on. He absolutely knew she would disapprove of the flat. The florist was getting her shop into readiness for the first plants and flowers and still working late into the evenings. Nick drew a breath of relief she was still there. The shabby door and uncarpeted stairs were as he had first seen them. Penny climbed them, holding her dress well away from

73

the walls. Nick unlocked his inner door and stepped back to let her view the interior. Tom had made amazing progress in the weeks since Nick had signed the agreement. The room was clean, the top coat of paint was on the woodwork, the walls colour-washed and all the ceilings white. Carpeted in a faded green, with a variety of chairs and a table it was all Nick needed. Tom had even made a start on the kitchen tiles. There was a long pause. Eventually, Penny spoke, "Nick, this is never going to be suitable. Could you honestly not find something more, more…"

"Appropriate?" Nick finished for her, smiling. She nodded. "No, though I undoubtedly could have done if I'd waited a bit. I just fell in love with this lovely large room. You should see it in daylight when the sun is out. I've been sleeping here for ages now as you know." Reluctantly, he showed her the kitchen and bedroom.

Penny remained unimpressed. "Nick, you'll have to think again. It's not at all suitable." Nick shrugged his shoulders and made to get into the car.

Later after a meal of roasted Camembert with a salad, halibut in a wonderful sauce followed by panna cotta and berries, they reached the coffee stage. Penny had enjoyed a gin and tonic in the lounge while they had waited to be called to their table. Nick had had a tomato juice, keeping to his one wine rule for the dining room. It was a beautiful seventeenth-century inn, well preserved and extended. Nick guessed the gardens would be beautiful in summer. The long windows were now curtained in heavy red brocade. Nick had his one glass of Sancerre, while Penny had a half bottle of something sweeter.

Penny stirred a lump of sugar into her coffee and lifted her face to look straight at Nick. "Now, come on, Nick. Tell me something about yourself. You must have had girlfriends, parents and a life apart from being at school with Ikbal and spending a year in Jordon? You're very difficult to get to know."

This was not a conversation Nick was prepared for, nor wanted. Penny was, perhaps, a little more relaxed with the wine, else he doubted she would have been quite so direct. He grimaced. "Actually, there's not a lot worth telling. My parents died shortly after I was born. For the first few years, I was brought up by a lovely couple and then I went to my even more lovely grandparents who took charge of my education and sent me to Postams. I loved medical school but basically, I'm a bit shy and have always run away from any socialising. I've really been too busy. I feel a bit about medicine as you do about your rallies, and felt I should give something to the world effort." Nick seemed to have reached a full stop but Penny was having none of it.

"What on earth possessed you to go to Jordon?" She asked, determined to get more out of him.

Nick shrugged. "There was a notice on the board at the hospital in Croydon asking for help in Jordon, particularly for someone interested in obstetrics. I'd just finished my three-year postgraduate stint and two years in 'obs and gynae' and decided to apply." He didn't qualify it by saying he had hoped it would let him escape for a while. If only the nightmares would then leave him. He'd now had enough of being questioned and reciprocated. "My turn," he said. "Tell me about your activities. They seem at variance with your lifestyle and background."

75

Penny's face lit up. "Well, it depends on which one you mean. I told you BAME was because of Ikbal but long before that I had got involved in the Labour Party and gender equality and xenophobia." She stopped for breath. "Each cause needs the support of people like me, just to show we are all hating the problems they find and are actually doing something about it. We don't just do rallies, you know."

Nick also took a deep breath. "You amaze me. One minute you're drinking with massively over rich friends, where I think you look familiar, comfortable and happy and the next, you are down to earth, a thinking and caring person trying to put the world to rights. I'm finding it difficult to connect the two 'you's'."

"Yes, I guess it is," Penny replied, "a bit like finding a refuse collector in the House of Lords. He might do a great job but he'd never be really comfortable. My parents inherited a sizeable amount of money and a title. They live lavishly. Father is a diplomat and we've lived in several countries at one time or another. I was sent to boarding school in a convent but I was always with them during school holidays. I learnt a lot about true values at school, if not taking the religious bit on board. My parents were not exactly delighted when I chose medicine. They wanted a suitable son-in-law and grandchildren. However, they were, and are always there for me." She stopped suddenly. "Golly, I've said a lot about me." Nick grinned. The last thing he wanted was for the conversation to come back to him but Penny got on first. "I did want to know about your romantic background, you are so good-looking, there must have been girlfriends? Are you good in bed? Have you got one tucked away somewhere now?"

Nick decided he had had enough. She had drunk an after-dinner brandy and was trying to be very seductive, making sure he could see right down her cleavage. He changed the subject abruptly. "No comment, I'm afraid. I keep my private life under wraps. Much more interesting, you tell me when is your next rally?"

Reluctantly, looking sulky, she abandoned his questioning. "It's next Sunday. Also in London. This is climate change. If ever I have children or grandchildren, I would be terrified of what will be happening in the world for them. We've permission to present a petition to Whitehall. Why don't you come? There are a super bunch who come in the coach. You'd get to now a whole new crowd."

Nick shook his head. "No, I cannot. Firstly, it's not my sort of thing. Secondly, I'm don't particularly want to get to know more people at the moment and thirdly, I need to get on with my flat or it'll never get finished."

"OK," replied Penny grudgingly, "we'll leave it there but I'll get you involved in something. You're too good to be wasted."

Nick again hastily changed the subject. "Tell me what you are doing about gender equality. Where do you look for it and what do you do about it?"

"Again, I could go on forever," Penny replied slowly, "but we're just about the last people here and I guess they'd like us to go. One quick example. You will always be addressed as 'doctor'. Two lines down in a letter I become Miss or Ms. If I marry, I guess it will be dropped immediately. Bit exaggerated but you watch. And that is the least serious we try to address. By letter, text, email or in person."

They drove to Penny's home in comparative silence. As he opened her door, she begged, "Come on Nick, just for once let go and come in for a drink before you go home? You could always sleep in the spare bed if you don't want to drink and drive."

Nick shook his head. "Thanks, but no. My grandparents will be expecting me home early tomorrow. I try to spend weekends visiting them."

"Gosh, it'll be good when you begin to feel properly independent. You must feel very tied."

He replied stonily, "Not really. It's been a great evening. And the meal I thought was perfect." He had recognised Penny's disdain and unspoken criticism. He admitted to himself there was a certain lack of truth in his excuses and, perhaps, they were a bit feeble.

After a short pause, Penny said brightly, "Thanks a million, Nick, it was lovely." She gave him a peck on the cheek and hurried, a little unsteadily, up the steps with her key at the ready. Nick waited for the house lights to come on before he drove off, thoughtfully. It had been a very expensive evening. Penny could never cope with his bogies. There was something phoney about her enthusiasms. Nor did he want that sort of independence.

Chapter 10
An Unusual Problem

Nick was even more pleased with the flat when it was finally finished and furnished. Apart from buying brightly coloured grass green flowered curtains, or rather the material which Emma made up for him, everything he could possibly need was found in the barn. The curtains left there were far too heavy and dark. Even a cooker and a washing machine were there. He proudly took Jane along one lunchtime to show how much it had improved since her last visit. She was delighted and asked if he would mind if Tim, the estate agent came and had a look. He too, was delighted. "My boy," he said, patting Nick's shoulder, "you've made the place habitable. Would like to suggest I can have the use of your grandfather."

"Too late!" exclaimed Nick happily. "He met a whole lot of new people when he was doing this job and has taken on a job of 'Mr Fixit' for the charity groups here. He gets asked to do things a couple of times most weeks. Gives him a real purpose for living."

For the first time, Nick had time to reflect. Charles had never asked how he was getting on with finding his father's background. He decided to make a start, probably duplicating what Yuri was doing. He had written two letters rather than emails or phone calls and enclosed copies of his birth certificate, driving licence and invoice for his present address, hoping to authenticate his enquiries. Both came to roost on the same day. He could not pluck up the courage to open either but left them on the table until the evening. It was not easy working, knowing there might be some answers in those letters. If he knew his father's name, he might be able to find death certificates to match both of them. It surprised him how much he needed to know. It seemed such an important part of his identity. He had watched others consult genealogists and inwardly thought it a waste of good time. Now, realising how much it meant he could fully understand and glad he had Yuri to sort it out. His grandparents must know from the work their researcher did. But he couldn't ask.

He opened the one from the Essex based social services first. He was bitterly disappointed. He had been literally just left on the doorstep with a card stating his name Nicholas, and a birth date on it. He had been six days old. They still had the card if he would like to collect it in person. He was wrapped in a towel with an imprinted name on it from a one-star London hotel, so soiled it was immediately destroyed. He resolved one day to collect the card. They also added a full police search had found no trace of his mother. Until a full legal right came to taking the swab for a DNA test, they knew nothing more but were delighted to hear the outcome. He could vaguely remember during his rebellious phase being made to listen to the fact he might have a relative and would he agree to the test. He had regarded it as a joke at the time but complied.

The second was marginally more helpful. And at least gave him a jumping-off point. Nathaniel Greenthorn was admitted to the medical school in 1968 and was in the same year as Mary Grovenor. Both had left after 2½ years. Mary had held the first-year medal for overall achievement and the Philip Purcell prize for physiology. Nathaniel the Doror prize in anatomy. He seemed to have come from very bright parents. Mary was admitted from Postams school in Norfolk, Nathaniel from a sixth form college in Islington. The address was included. Nick deduced his father was a Londoner. Briefly, he searched the internet for the sixth form college in question, only to find it had been demolished in 1980 to be amalgamated with another. His home address was also not there. He'd try but that route looked shut to him. He began to wonder if he should follow his grandparents and leave it all to the professionals.

Firstly, he wanted sight of the death certificates. Greenthorn was not a common name. That might be more helpful but try as he might he could find no one of that name. Maybe he made it up and had done a change by deed poll.

While mulling this over the next morning during a mid-morning break, Nick was half listening to an animated conversation between Maria and Gerry over their coffee. He was alerted when the subject turned to 'detransition'. Now an everyday word, it had been new to him when he first found it on a revision programme. He had come across the term in a medical update course and had needed to look it up. So, he was a little surprised to hear it again in an ordinary interchange. It meant 'to revert a person to his or her original gender after that person had received gender altering treatment or surgery'. Maria was saying, sounding a bit desperate, "I just don't know where to go next. Whatever I say is wrong and he or she bursts into tears."

Gerry looked sympathetic. "I realise where you are coming from. I had one consultation and he rushed out shouting I was too old hat to understand what it was all about. And even added that I probably hated him."

Nick interrupted, "Better not let Penny in on that. She might not approve at all. But, seriously, if I can help. Do let me see him. I attended a refresher course recently at my old medical school and that was one of the major topics. I don't pretend to do the essential job of the psychologists trained in this area but I did learn a lot of the pointers, what not to say and where to refer for specialist care or surgery. I can probably dig it out on my laptop if it's any help."

"Would you?" asked Maria gratefully. "I suppose it's my rigid RC background but even if I know it's quite correct and should be normal and acceptable, I must send out the wrong vibes."

Charles looked across at Nick. "If you can handle Hilary's massive problem, I reckon we'll all be grateful; he's been in and out of the surgery for the last couple of months and never left content or accepting available offers of help."

"Before I do, has Penny seen him?" he asked. "This should be right up her street. I'd have thought she knew more about it than any of us."

"I believe so," answered Charles levelly, "but I think she may have been over the top a little. He told her a few home truths about it, I fear. The consultation did not end happily. He is a Cambridge maths graduate, so it's no good telling him what he already knows."

Nick nodded thoughtfully. "Thanks for that bit of information. Does help one to prepare a little."

Two days later, the surgery having made an appointment for him, Hilary came into Nick's consulting room. He was slight in stature, not much over five foot six. Another redhead like himself but longer hair tied back in a loose ponytail. A suggestion of a downy beard and a mass of freckles. Dressed in a grubby black sleeveless T-shirt, despite the chill in the air, and equally grubby jeans, it was difficult for Nick to believe he had an intelligent person in front of him. The introductory words didn't help either. In a gravelly voice, he stated, rather than spoke, without looking at Nick, "Can't think why you'll be any bloodier good than the rest of your stupid crew. All they can think of is where they can refer me and then all to the wrong people. I know. I've bloody been there." He bent over, tapping his knees impatiently staring at the floor. Nick stared at him silently until Hilary, at last, looked up and faced him.

"I have absolutely no doubt you have researched the whole thing to a point beyond which we GPs cannot possibly go," Nick spoke slowly and quietly. "I realise you want something different from sick notes, platitudes and being told where to go. Right?" Hilary stared at Nick.

"God," he said, "a doctor who talks sense. First time in this shop I've met one!" Nick grinned. "Must be the red hair. Look, I'm fairly new here. I do not know what you know. I need to start at the beginning and learn who you are."

"Blimey! We'll be here forever if we start there."

"OK," said Nick, "let's get going. We haven't quite got forever, Also, I'm well aware you have been through all this questionnaire stuff many times before. You should have it nicely abbreviated by now." Hilary had been a typical tomboy, better at sciences and maths and misread the signals as permanent. To cut a long story short, he had changed from girl to boy grammar schools and started on the necessary sex hormone drugs. Nick interrupted the flow. "Stop, just there, please. Go back to the moment you realised your gender was wrong, and tell me why you felt the need to be a boy."

"My parents were like any other, so utterly bemused they took me to our GP who referred me to the Tavistock. After that, they just stood by and took me where I needed to go. No, I wasn't actually bullied. I had great difficulty making a real friend. I was too used to my brothers for girl's company. If girl's football had been around then, I might have survived. I just couldn't settle. My body was just beginning to change shape and I couldn't cope with it. I guess part of me didn't want to grow up. I kept applying bandages to my chest to keep it flat. I became almost anorectic. I was 13 when I was first referred for evaluation. I have to admit, they were very thorough indeed and after a couple of years both I and they thought I did indeed need to change my gender. I was started on male hormones and for a time felt really happy. With my hair cropped, I did indeed look more boy than a girl. I sailed through the next four years at school and by all sorts of devious methods escaped loo and undressing problems. Of necessity, I developed a hatred of games." Hilary was gradually relaxing and losing the initial aggressiveness. "At Cambridge, I met others who had had gender changes. Wonderful. A fellowship. In the second long vacation, I took the big step to have both breasts removed. I think it was now, when I think rationally, that step was the one that was one step too far. Depression set in. I ended up with a 2:2 when I should easily have got a first and been invited to stay on. Tried doing a post-grad teaching in maths but couldn't stand the stupidity of some children. Dropped out. Have never really worked since. Got it? And the solution? Every time I tell someone how utterly miserable, I am and that all I want to do is cry, they offer me anti-depressants."

"Well, I'll not bother with that then!" said Nick decisively. "Now. Tell me three good reasons why you want to be female."

Hilary didn't hesitate for long. "Firstly, I held my baby nephew for the first time nearly a year ago and I ache all over wanting a baby. I had thought the testosterone would have done that. It doesn't. Secondly, it hurt where my breasts should have been. Even if I detransition, I'll never be able to do that. Thirdly, and I suppose this is the important bit. I tried both sorts of relationships and sex at Cambridge and just none of them seemed right. The only chap I ever met into whose arms I would gladly have wallowed was a proper heterosexual male. I still ache for him too. Satisfied?" Hilary looked defiantly at Nick. Eventually, he took up the conversation again. "You're right. I need to get on with it. Why, in the name of all that's good and great, do they let kids make such decisions?"

Nick replied gently, "A few kids do need it but I think most could wait many more years. But please, don't stop hormone treatment without professional help, will you?" Hilary got up, grabbed Nick's hand in a quick handshake and walked rapidly out of the room.

Having run late as usual, Nick realised he would have to speed up a bit. It might be a country town practice but it was not at the slow Norfolk pace. Just time to snatch a coffee. He had almost forgotten there was time set aside for a practice meeting. The sounds of an animated discussion met him long before he reached the room. Jane was quietly taking notes, listening to it all. Nick slid in beside her and asked what it was all about. "Oh," she whispered, "the annual argument about where to have the Christmas lunch." She pulled a face. "We'll end up in the Bull as usual. You watch." He cut across the room to rescue a coffee.

Penny appealed to him, "Nick, which do you think is most important, the food, ambience or cost?"

Put on the spot he gave a hasty reply, "I've no idea! I've sat through a couple. Depends who it's for. If it's to say thank you to the staff, I reckon ambience and a chance to chat is the most important. If it's for the doctors to enjoy a good nosh up, then that must be number one. I have no idea what's on offer."

Charles chuckled. "Out of the mouth of babes...sorry, Nick but that was it in a nutshell."

"You've let me down, Nick," Penny wailed, "I dislike the Bull. We go there every year and it's the same and the same dry turkey and solid Christmas pudding and veggie choices so uninteresting."

"But," Maria interrupted, "it's always a success, everyone laughs, there are plenty of chances to circulate, and if you must, to dance."

Charles turned to Jane. "Jane, The Bull it is. Please will you do your usual and book us up?" She nodded, turned to Nick and winked. It was so good just to sit near him. When would he find out what Penny was like? Penny would do her usual trick of leading him on until she got tired, and then just drop him. And he would be hurt. He was worth a hundred times more than she was. Her heart didn't stop racing when he was close by, or she even thought about him. It had never occurred to her it was possible to love more than once. Robin had been so very, very special. Nick, as far as she could see thought of her as part of the furniture.

Nick, having resumed his seat next to Jane turned to her. "As I've indicated before, I hate Christmas lunches, or dinners or social occasions. It's not what I was designed to do. I only enjoy one drink and the pressure is always on to drink more. Guess I'm not allowed to escape?"

Jane replied, animatedly, "No, you are jolly well not! If I have to go, so do you. And I never drink, so end up wallowing in orange juice. And you need to be cheerful, laugh at cracker jokes, tell the staff how wonderful they are, be polite to your colleagues and then get up on the dance floor at the end!"

"No!" he exclaimed firmly. "That I do draw the line at. To be honest, I cannot and have not a clue how to. I would hate to display my ignorance." Jane giggled. The meeting had been drawn to order. There were finances, procedures and other matters to discuss.

Afterwards, Penny grabbed him by the arm. "How did your consultation go with Hilary?"

Nick hesitated. "I…I think well enough. He seems to have found his own ability to make a decision, with a good idea of moving forwards instead of looking backwards. I didn't know you had seen him."

"Oh, yes," Penny said, "it was right up my street and I saw him leaving your room. He should have come back to me and I would have helped more. I've met so many transitions on our rallies and they're so glad to be liberated; if only society would accept them." Nick looked puzzled. "But his problem is he is not happy with the decision he has made and has asked for help."

"No, no, I don't think he is disappointed. Just needs help with adjustment."

Penny replied shaking her head hard, "I feel strongly he needs to discuss those issues with other transitions long before deciding to go backwards." Nick shrugged, pulled away from her grasp and went back to his consulting room. Yet again, he wondered just how she ticked. Or perhaps it was he who had misread the problem?

Chapter 11
Is There a Doctor in the House?

Nick's life was beginning to settle into a routine. Now a member of the Cromer and District Choral Society, he was really looking forward to the Christmas concerts. He'd already given his grandparents tickets. He had tried persuading Penny to come to one but she felt it was the sort of music she couldn't enjoy. There was something anyway about Penny he didn't want to introduce to his grandparents. He was in fact greatly relieved.

He had asked his grandparents to let him have his mother's piano in his flat. After Mary was presumed dead, they had had it removed to the back of an old disused barn. The piano held far too many reminders of happier days. It took a pair of professional movers to get it up the stairs. Tom had French polished it, almost back to its original beauty. A local piano tuner had succeeded in repairing and tuning it. No near neighbours, so he could enjoy making as much noise as he liked without disturbing anyone.

The florist shop was now up and really flourishing. It was good to see her working all hours to get her displays and bouquets out in time for Christmas. On one of the rare occasions when they met, she declared she might be able to afford some help if Christmas proved as good as it looked to be.

Sundays were spent with the grandparents every week giving him an absolutely iron-clad reason why he could never go to any of the Penny's rallies. The latest one for Me2 seemed rather out of date but it obviously still went deeply with a lot of women. One part of Nick admired her passion for those who were in need, and causes but the other part wondered quite why she needed to get so involved in so many causes. Her friend, who had mocked his ginger hair, had been arrested for refusing to get out of a road block and then drawing blood on a policeman by scratching. He just couldn't see the point. But women, he supposed, would never have achieved a vote without such heroics. It was always with same the wealthy, highly educated crowd and to Nick, felt phoney.

Very sensibly, the places for the Christmas dinner at The Bull were all named. Jane did this, spacing the doctors out among the staff. Nick liked that idea. After each course, the doctors were expected to move round one. There was no room for any cliques or the 'must sit by' cries which inevitably occur on such occasions. The large, low room was beautifully decorated, as were the tables. The atmosphere was cheerful and noisy with staff finding their places and greeting their neighbours. Perhaps, Nick thought, this was not going to be too bad after all. It was Friday and he had planned to go home immediately afterwards as various members of the family were gathering for lunch on Saturday. Emma had been cooking for weeks to prepare for it and wanted Nick back to help move furniture around to make space for them all. This just might allow him to get away early.

However, much to his surprise, he found he was actually enjoying himself. Having watched Tom slaughter his home-grown turkeys in preparation for the Saturday gathering, he had opted for the vegetarian main course. The nut roast not only looked good but to his surprise, actually tasted really good. The salmon starter had been a bit ordinary but very nice. Jose, the diminutive receptionist he had first met was next to him with Liz and her husband, directly opposite. This made chatting very easy. Liz was obviously trying hard to make up for her previous frostiness. Undoubtedly, on reflection, she had realised it was typical of Penny. She had known her for long enough to see how her selfish mind worked.

Just then, as Charles was about to stand up and tell all the doctors to move round one, the bar man, who turned out to be the landlord, came in and whispered something to Charles, which sounded like, "Is there a doctor in the house?" There was a ripple of laughter from those who overheard the whisper. Charles eventually pointed a finger at Nick indicating he should go with the landlord. Puzzled, Nick got up, had his arm firmly grabbed and almost frogmarched towards the ladies' toilet, the landlord explaining as he went, he understood someone was having a baby 'in there'. There was a very agitated group standing outside. A slightly slurred voice asked, "Are you the doctor?"

A somewhat frantic tall dark-haired, a young man dressed very smartly in a dark blue suit rushed forwards to meet him. Barely able to get his words out, he eventually managed to tell Nick, "She's not due for another three weeks and it's our first anniversary." He gulped and struggled to continue. "Says her waters have gone, or something." It was apparent he had already been celebrating hard.

"I am," replied Nick sounding far more confident than he felt. Premature babies in a nice safe hospital environment were one thing here in a loo was something different. Even in Jordon, there had been a sort of hospital. Though, this just couldn't be anything as bad as he had faced many times there, he still reckoned this was awkward in the extreme. "Has someone called an ambulance?"

A burly chap intervened. "Yeah. Says it's Friday and it's busy." Nick went through the swing door into a small handwashing area. One distraught girl was sitting on the loo, with an older woman, who looked so like her it had to be her mother, holding her hand and keeping the door open. The place reeked of alcohol.

"First of all," said Nick, far more authoritatively than he felt, "get off the loo. Better to have a mess on the floor than a baby to rescue from the loo. Just squat for a minute. He poked his head outside the door and spoke to the hovering landlord. Please, as fast as you can, towels and if possible, blankets or sheets. No good the rest of you standing there. One of you get outside and guide the ambulance men or responders or whoever comes here as fast as possible." He added angrily, "And then get out of the way!" He went back inside. She was very controlled, sweating and trying not to yell out. The wine intake was taking some of the pain out of the situation. "Good lass," said Nick quietly, "just don't push and try to hang on until we get something a little cleaner to lay you on. Mother?" She nodded biting her lips together. "Please could you tuck yourself into the second loo so I have a bit more room?" The door opened; a big pile of towels was thrust at him. Carefully, he laid them out and let her lie down. "Not very comfortable, I realise." Nick attempted a grin. "Just let me wash my hands

92

as best I can, then we'll try and find out whether you can get to the hospital in time, or whether we have it just here. Girl or boy?"

"Girl," – She panted between contractions – "I'm Elaine." There was no need to ask any further questions. It needed all Nick's skill to stop Elaine from pushing too quickly and causing brain damage to the baby, and damage to herself. He thought Elaine looked more than three weeks premature. Elaine certainly had not planned to have her baby in such an embarrassing place. Then there was one big yell and the baby emerged, guided slowly by Nick. There was a brief knock on the door. A paramedic poked his nose around and instantly grasped the situation. By the time he had gone back to the car for his equipment, the new mother herself, who couldn't have been more than in her late teens, was sitting, leaning against the wall, radiantly holding the tiny infant wrapped in a towel. Her mother looked as concerned as Nick felt.

The paramedic came back. "Have you any ergometrine or similar? And do you carry it and something to tie off the cord on the baby? Then I'll hand over to you." Once the placenta was delivered, and it took its time, Nick rose from his uncomfortable position and gratefully handed over baby, Elaine and the mess to the experts.

After a wash and brush up in one of the upstairs bedrooms, Nick went back to the dining room hoping someone had saved him his pudding. By this time, most had gone home. The landlord was fulsome in his thanks promising Nick free meals and whatever he could want. Sadly, the pudding had gone back to the kitchen and was no more. Charles had waited to find out how things went and, like Nick, hoped the baby would arrive in the premature baby unit in time. There was a small group at the end of one of the tables finishing a bottle of wine. Penny, of course, was among them, now much the worse for wear. Charles asked, "Nick, have you got your car here? I know you'd planned to go to the farm. Could you take Penny home? I'd rather not get a taxi for her as I know her parents are back."

Nick sighed. He was tired and he still had a half-hour drive ahead of him. Reluctantly, he unearthed his iPhone from his inner pocket. "I'll ring gran and tell her I'm going to be late." He walked over to the table and peremptorily told Penny to get her wrap and come out to the car. Unsteadily, she did as she was told, meanwhile singing to herself. They drove in silence while she giggled. The house was ablaze with lights. Nick helped her up the steps and rang the bell. The door was answered by a tall austere looking woman who assessed the situation in a glance.

"Bring her in and take her upstairs."

Nick had had enough. "Sorry, I'm just the driver. You'll have to look after her yourselves."

"Oh…Nick." Penny started crying. "You've got to come up and see me into bed."

"No, I haven't," said Nick. "I've got a long drive home."

With that, a very formal, tall, extremely handsome older man came to the door. "Well-spoken young man. You must be Nick. You sound like the first sensible chap she's ever had. I really want to meet you. Drinks here, Tuesday evening at 6. Need to say thank you. Promise to come?" Nick would have given anything he possessed to say no but he desperately wanted his bed at the farm, so he just nodded.

Chapter 12
Jane and Emily

Nick slept fitfully, he was overtired, worried about the very floppy premature baby, worrying about his relationship with Penny and above all dreading Tuesday evening. What on earth did one wear to that sort of event? Would Penny wait for him? Over and over his mind refused to let go. He knew he should never have committed himself but equally knew once, having made a promise, he would have to. Before 7 am, he was aware of Emma bustling noisily about in the kitchen indicating clearly to Nick she wanted him up and helping. He dragged himself out of bed, donned a dressing gown and slippers and made his way down. "Good morning, Nick," she greeted him a little coldly. "Tea's in the teapot and while you're waiting for it to cool, would you reach me down those puddings from the top shelf in the larder. I'd right like to get them on as quickly as possible. The longer they cook, the better they are." There was a moment's hesitation. "Must have been a good do last evening. You were late enough." She sniffed.

"Sorry, Gran, hope I didn't keep you up. Some poor lady had a premature baby in the middle of our meal. No, not one of our patients but a pub client, in the loo of all places, and it took time before the ambulance arrived. Then one of our doctors had too much to drink, so needed taking home."

Emma had stopped bustling. "Why you? And did you miss your tea? And was it a boy or a girl?"

Nick pulled a face. "I'm the only one with recent birthing qualifications. It was a very small little girl. I might ring up to see how she is later on. Worst of all, my one and only suit is a mess and I'm due at a horribly formal party on Tuesday. The landlord of the Bull has promised to see to it for me but I do need to take it in today. Is there anything you need in Mersham when I pop in?"

Emma relaxed. "Hm. Yes, I'd like some fancy chocolates. Yes, I know you'll tell me that at least one of them will bring some but I'd like them in case. But you'll get all the tables ready first, won't you? Then you can get lost until midday."

Having delivered his suit, Nick was walking back to his flat mulling over the dreaded coming Tuesday evening. He hoped a fleeting appearance would be all that was needed. He absolutely knew he would be tongue-tied when confronted with the austere looking woman or her imperious husband. He was so deep in his miseries he almost knocked Jane over. The town was heaving with Christmas shoppers and he was taking no notice of where he was going. "You look as if the cares of the world are on your shoulders." Laughed Jane.

Nick grimaced. "Well, they are but we've got a lovely family lunch today so I must get my act together. I think Gran is cooking for 16 of us."

Just then a little girl pulled on Jane's sleeve and piped up. "Mummy, Mummy, you promised me if I came shopping with you, I could have a treat."

Nick stepped to one side to avoid yet another pull along trolley. "Ah," he said to the child conversationally, trying to disguise his surprise, "now who are you? Am I right? Are you really Flopsy Bunny?" She gave a lovely giggle. Not a particularly attractive child, until her face lit up. A very thin nine-year-old with an oval face like her mother's, an olive complexion, long black curly hair tied back in bunches and dark brown eyes.

"Nick, this is my daughter, Emily. Yes, I did promise you a treat," replied Jane, "but it's really too crowded to try and eat an ice cream here. It would get knocked out of your hand in minutes. Let's wait until we're home, shall we?"

Nick observed Emily's downcast face and interrupted impulsively, "Look, why don't Emily and I go across to Marigold's and choose that fabulous ice cream for her and then we'll bring it back to my flat to eat it? Emily, I'll give Mum the key and she might just be able to find a kettle and put it on for some coffee for us dull grown-ups. Actually, Jane, I don't think you've seen it since it was properly furnished, have you?" Jane, looking slightly discomfited, nodded, took the key and went in the direction of the flat.

Meanwhile, Emily took Nick's hand and dancing up and down went with him across the road. "You're Nick, aren't you?" Emily looked up at him. "Mummy says you're nice. I like your red hair. Much better than black," she said wistfully.

"Don't you believe it," Nick retorted, "Most people think it's funny. Would you like to be called 'carrots'?" Emily was silent. "Now, which ice cream would you like?"

"Can I really, really choose?"

Nick replied solemnly, "I've given my word. You can."

"Then I'll have that one. Please?" She pointed to the displayed picture of a giant chocolate covered one on a stick. By now they had reached the head of the queue. Nick chose a couple of fancy cakes, handed the ice cream to Emily and both walked carefully across the road dodging other walkers, cyclists and cars.

Meanwhile, Jane had successfully made coffee and even found the tray and mugs. She was sitting at the piano trying to sight-read the music already on the piano. "I had no idea you played," she said as she got down from the stool and sat in an armchair. Nick grabbed a plate and handed Jane a cake to go with the coffee. "This is really lovely," she said admiringly. "The room is so complete now, comfortable and friendly. You are full of surprises. Bach is probably my all-time favourite composer but I've never attempted to play much by him. Just about can manage *Jesu joy of man's desiring* badly. Singing yes. Clarinet, yes. Every time."

Nick rushed to get a tea towel to mop up Emily just as the ice cream gradually melted and was about to descend into her lap. "My real aim is to play the organ properly," Nick said dreamily, "but so far have not found time to go and find an organ for practice, nor a good teacher."

Jane said thoughtfully, "I think I can help you with both those but let me do a little research first."

They had quite forgotten Emily. "Mummy, why is our piano still in the front room where we can't get at it? There are chairs and boxes and so many things in there."

Jane replied quietly, "Mainly because I cannot move all that stuff and for various reasons, I have never got around to sorting it."

Quite spontaneously, Nick butted in, "Can I help with that? To be without a piano if you're trying to practise singing must be difficult?"

Jane shook her head slowly. "That is a very kind offer but I must refuse. I cannot ask you to do that," Jane replied firmly. "Now, before we go, why were you looking so miserable when we met?" Briefly, he related the story, unwittingly disclosing his developing low opinion of Penny. "Well, you are a silly chump! If you've only got one suit, forget it. Go in your casual gear. If you stick out like a sore thumb, enjoy it. You're worth hundreds of them. It's not worth a second thought. Penny is well known for her man-eating ways. Knowing you, if you've promised to go, you will. Else just forget the whole thing!"

Looking stunned, Nick thought for a minute. "Do you know, I am being as stupid as a nervous teenager. Thanks a million. I feel so much better now."

It had been such a natural interlude and both had been completely comfortable with it. Nick drove back to the farm feeling light-hearted for the first time in weeks. Again, he wondered if she did have a husband at home. She never mentioned him, and Emily had never mentioned her father. She wouldn't be divorced, or she would have removed the ring. Every time he thought of a home with a wife and family, he became aware it was Jane's face he kept seeing. Shaking his head hard, he could never let her know. He must not fall in love with a married woman. This feeling of completeness, the only word he could think of, was so utterly different from what he felt for Penny. It could only lead to unhappiness. Jane returned home with her heart aching with love for this man. Emily had found someone to hero-worship.

The chocolates had been forgotten.

It was a few minutes after 12 when he arrived but Tom's brother had arrived with his family in tow; the noise was really rising, and already on the table were two large boxes of chocolates. Nick heave a sigh of relief and Gran was too busy cooking and talking to notice his omission.

Chapter 13
A Diplomatic Incident

Jane may have cheered Nick up but Tuesday dawned, and he was filled with apprehension for the evening. Whatever Jane may have said, the parents were probably good and genuine people. They would never have survived in the very complex diplomatic world otherwise. Also, he guessed they were now finding their very spoilt daughter worrying. As Nick supposed most of the guests would be their choice, not Penny's, they would also be genuinely nice people. He knew full well the only differences from him would be their privileged upbringing and that substance called money. That was not his fault but he would wear his suit and be as polite as possible. Afterwards, he would tell Penny he would tell her any relationship they had was over. He would be lonely for a bit, he knew but this was more than he could take.

Tuesday seemed to be filled with all the heart-sink patients, those who came over and over again for no discernible reason, the over-anxious, the sore throats and colds that 'must be better by Christmas' and even his two visits were unnecessary. However, coming Wednesday, he would have a whole day to himself, and that dreaded evening would be over. He needed a couple of days helping at home and to get his own Christmas shopping done. Usually, surgeries became less pressurised as the long holiday season approached. Patients were far too busy with shopping and preparations to come to the surgery. He hoped to get into Norwich. There was a carol concert he hoped to get to on Thursday. Friday there was to be a buffet lunch brought in for staff and doctors, courtesy of Charles. There was a need to buy a present under £10 for the person he had drawn out of the hat. The idea was he or she should be able to guess who the donor was. Oddly, he had drawn Jane. Not too difficult!

It was a lovely crisp evening with a nearly full moon. Not that it needed much lightning with all the Christmas ones across the street and in the shops. Nick decided to walk the half mile or so. He felt it might embarrass him to park his car amongst the chauffeured ones. His dark grey suit, now superbly cleaned and pressed, pale blue shirt and discrete medical school tie made him feel comfortable. He polished his black shoes until they shone. A rare occurrence.

The semi-circular entrance was parked nose to tail with expensive cars. A number of top range Lexus among them. Drivers were standing around smoking and chatting. He was obviously not the first there. With some trepidation, he rang the bell. It was answered immediately by, presumably, the butler. He was ushered in; his long anorak removed and then ushered up the first flight of stairs. There were upwards of 30 people already holding glasses and chatting to each other in a massive drawing room. There were open fires at both ends of the richly carpeted, brightly lit room. Penny's father walked towards him with a very friendly smile, accompanied by his wife who also seemed pleased to meet him. She called for Penny, asking her to come as soon as she saw Nick arrive.

Penny was at his side in extra quick time, giving Nick a strong feeling her mother was not one to be trifled with. For some five minutes, they chatted easily about Mersham, the school he had attended and his time at medical school. All so easy. Of course, Nick told himself, he'd been absolutely stupid to worry. These people were used to conversing with the whole range of human diversity from the queen to the itinerant, making them feel inclusive. Interrupting their conversation, there was a noticeable, sudden and complete silence throughout the room. A young man of some 30 years, Mediterranean in appearance, in an immaculate Saville row suit walked in. Not tall but completely arresting, with piercing eyes and longish hair well brushed back. He made an impressive entrance. Everyone took a step back from him. His presence filled the room. Besides Nick, Penny quietly slid to the floor. Utterly bemused, he lay her down more comfortably, checked her pulse and knelt beside her. Gradually she revived, clutched Nick convulsively and hysterically asked him not to leave her. Meanwhile, the centre of attention had moved from the young man to Penny. The room remained absolutely silent. "Good Evening all." He looked around the assembled company with a sneer. "So nice to be made welcome." His voice was heavily accented. Italian, Nick guessed. "But it's been a long time since you have all seen me, isn't it?" His gaze went around the room again, and then stopped, fixed on Penny. "Don't worry, I won't be long. I've just come to claim my son. And Penny if she doesn't prefer this carrot-top, as I think you would call him." Nick flushed scarlet.

The incomer glared angrily at Nick. "You take her to bed then, do you? Hey?"

Nick shook his head, meanwhile regaining his composure. He replied quietly but with surprising authority, "Penny is a colleague and friend." Furious at the taunt, he added with his voice rising, "No more than that but I will stand by her if you are causing trouble."

A booming voice said, "The rest of us should resume our conversation from where we left off. Fabio and Penny will sort their problem out in private. I suggest, Fabio, you take Penny into the second drawing room over there." He pointed.

"No, Nick," Penny's father said forcefully, "there is no need for you to accompany Penny. Penny will be quite safe here." Fabio grabbed Penny's arm in a vicious grip. She could barely stand. Nick had been holding her up. Fabio muttered as he led her away, "If you took my son to that clinic, I might…I might kill you too." Meanwhile her father nodded to the butler who discretely entered the second drawing room quickly and quietly. Her father walked towards Nick. "Nick, I can only say how sorry I am you should be at all involved in this. The shock of seeing Fabio was a shock for all of us." He swallowed hard. Even his composure was ruffled. "He was sentenced in Italy nine years ago for 30 years in prison with no parole. His father was enormously important in Italian politics, and the rather uncouth son thought he should be too. He made serious blunders, ending in a man being killed. I think you are entitled to a bit of the story. Denise and John, here, might be willing to fill you in. I need to circulate more than ever. Please forgive me." Nick was by now speechless, completely stunned by the incident. John came and introduced himself and Denise. Both in their late 40s and he looked entirely Eton and Oxford-educated.

John spoke first, wryly, "I guess this is all a big surprise for you?"

Nick found his tongue. "Yes. Totally. Penny somehow never quite surprises me. But I'm totally bemused and embarrassed by the whole episode and just want to escape from here."

John nodded. "Bear with me for a moment if you will. I think you should understand a little of what has happened." This time it was Nick who gave a faint nod, shifted his feet unwillingly and looked steadily at John. "I was at the Embassy in Rome when we first came across Fabio senior. He was ultra-polished and very much a professional diplomat. And good at his job. Being naively British, I can't say I took the Mafia seriously but I and others, had reason to believe he was involved. Fabio junior took one look at Penny's golden hair and fair complexion and had her in bed in no time."

Here Denise interrupted. "We were all seriously worried about her welfare and tried to persuade Lady MacAulay to rein Penny in. I don't know what's wrong with some parents but they can see no wrong in their precious offspring. The affaire lingered on."

"I believe," John went on, "Penny had just finished either medical school or hospital jobs but she stayed in Italy for about six months. Wasn't it you, Denise, who first thought she was pregnant?"

Denise shook her head. "No, it was the nurse who looked after the welfare of the embassy staff who asked me to talk to her. I did. Days after Fabio was arrested for the murder of his father. Another long story of a family feud and young Fabio running into debt and his father refusing to pay. Penny fled

105

back to England and to fill her time with her work. We guessed she had aborted the baby."

Nick looked thoroughly discomforted, still doing his utmost to leave. "It is all completely outside my experience. He made such an impressive entrance I really thought it was an act. And you all stopped dead."

John nodded. "You see, we all had had contact with him in one way or another. In our diplomatic world, it is a reasonably small network. People like Fabio junior are apt to make waves. We each held great hopes they would hold him for the full 30 years. One day we may find out why not.

Denise spoke, "You know, John, if Lady MacAulay had had a whisper of suspicion Penny was pregnant, she would have somehow stopped it. She is an ardent Roman Catholic. He is not but he wouldn't approve in any way of a late abortion."

Nick shuddered. "I just hope she is safe with him," he said, "because I cannot wait to get out of here. You are all in a different world from mine. But thank you for taking the time away from your friends to fill me in. I am grateful."

John gave Nick a boyish grin. "And your world terrifies me. You deal daily with life and death and make decisions we would never contemplate. Don't ever underestimate your value for one minute. And don't worry about Penny. I saw Lord M's bodyguard step in."

Chapter 14
Nick Is Useful

Nick slept very fitfully and was glad when morning came. Instead of his planned home and shopping day, he knew the practice would be short of a doctor. They would need him. He could not imagine for one moment Penny would be in any shape or form to be fit for work that day, or in this surgery ever again. He had lost even the slightest attraction for her. Time and time again he had witnessed her not being one hundred percent genuine. Nick was genuinely, however, concerned about her safety and her future. It had all been so effortlessly smoothed over.

Next morning, Nick arrived at the staff entrance at the same time as Jane. Emily was with her. "Nick, Nick," she greeted him excitedly, "did you have a picture from Sophia stuck to your kitchen door?"

Collecting himself with some difficulty, he replied, "Er…yes. She spent a Saturday morning with me and drew that lovely picture then. Why? Are you going to draw one for me too? I'd like the one about…Christmas shopping? Or what you would like for Christmas?" Emily nodded happily.

"Holidays are always a bit of a problem," Jane said very quietly. "Maria is wonderful but I can't use her too often now.

But Emily is really good at entertaining herself and the nurses pop in and see her. Today it was going to be your room that was free. What on earth are you doing here? And how did you survive last evening? I thought you were supposed to be shopping."

Nick pulled a face and shook his head. "Let her use Penny's. I'll guarantee she won't be in today."

"Intriguing," said Jane enquiringly, "fill me in once I get this young lady settled."

Ten minutes later, Nick was seated in Jane's office. How comfortable, just to be with her. "Do you know, Jane, I can hardly expect you to believe any of this. I don't think I believe it myself. Before I tell Charles the saga, I'd be grateful for your impression. It's just so bizarre. I could dimly see it all happening, in a novel. Even then I'd find it far-fetched."

She sat silently whilst Nick tried to give an accurate account of his evening. After giving it serious thought, she said, "Nick, I've seen a lot of Penny over the years and to me, it doesn't sound as strange as it does to you. Sir Edward is well-liked by Charles, who regards both of them as the genuine article. Penny is extremely clever in languages, travel, world affairs as well as medicine. It all came too easily but with no real commitment to medicine. I know she has disappointed Charles and her parents on many occasions. You'd better go and see him before he starts and I'll get the girls organised on sending you her patients."

Charles too, was far less surprised by the story than Nick would have expected. When Nick expressed concern for Penny's safety, firstly having ensured Charles understood he no longer had any feeling for her, Charles scoffed at the idea. "Poof! Sir Edward has his own bodyguards on duty at all times, a private aeroplane at Norwich airport, a chauffeur at the ready, so I would guess she is way over the ocean in a place of safety. No worry. Don't look so surprised! It's how these people live. Sir Edward is and has been deeply involved in some dangerous diplomacy with very serious threats made against him. I've known them all my working life, been to certain of their gatherings and gradually discovered, as you have done, their utter disappointment in daughter Penelope. Relax, and oh, thanks a million times for coming in. We'll make sure you get tomorrow off."

Later that day, there was a hand-delivered letter to Nick. A thick pale grey envelope containing a single sheet of thick pale grey paper from Sir Edward and Lady MacAulay, headed with their Mersham address.

Dr Grovenor,

We are deeply indebted to you for your care and affection for Penelope over the last few months. We had indeed hoped for once, she had found someone of whom we could both approve. Indeed, we had made some effort to know more about you and would have been delighted if the relationship had continued. Our sincere concern you were subjected to such abuse yesterday evening.

However, as you discovered, she had flung herself at this man, Fabio, only a few months before he was arrested for the shooting of his father. His plea of murder has recently been overturned to the lesser one of manslaughter, hence his unexpected discharge from prison. Even in France, where the incident took place, I fear the Italian money played a part. The original verdict was beyond doubt.

Neither myself nor Lady MacAulay had the slightest idea Penelope was pregnant, or else we would have constrained her to keep the baby. My wife is a devout Roman Catholic, and whereas it is not my choice of religion, I would have stood firmly by her. Last evening, Penelope confessed she was four months into the pregnancy and a scan had confirmed it was a boy. When Fabio was committed to prison, she decided upon a termination. Whereas I can understand her reason, I cannot condone the action.

In conclusion, Dr Grovenor, please may I reassure you she is in a place of total safety but will not be able to contact you.

Nick's hands were shaking as he carefully folded the letter and took it into Charles for his perusal. It was late afternoon and with only two consultations left wished he had not opened it before he had finished.

Jane met him at the door as he was about to leave the building. "This has taken a lot out of you, hasn't it?" she inquired gently.

"It has," Nick confessed, "but I'm also feeling cross and angry. The MacAulays had been making enquiries about me to see if I were a suitable candidate for the hand of their daughter, Penelope. That is insufferable. Even if it's what people like that 'do'."

Jane looked quizzically at him. "Well, and what do you intend on doing about it? Complain?"

Nick relaxed and grinned. "Guess you are right, not a lot. I've put the letter on Charles's desk to seek his comments. He'll apply a little more soothing balm."

"Now," said Jane, "are you really going into Norwich tomorrow?"

Nick nodded. "Would you be prepared to pick up a parcel from John Lewis? I really would like Emily to have a real surprise for Christmas and she won't get one if I have to drag her into the city."

Nick's face lit up. "Great. I'd love to. What is it?"

"It's a puppet theatre with a couple of hand puppets and a couple of string ones to see if she is big enough to handle them. She's always making up stories and playing and getting her dolls to act them out."

"What fun! Presumably an Ikea type flat-pack?"

Jane nodded. "Now, I'd better go and see if Liz has had enough of her. I've still another hour or so to do today. Dear Penelope has really landed us in the cart."

Impulsively, Nick offered, "Would you like me to take her off your hands for an hour or so? I need to go back to the grandparents to sort my room as my Aunt from Bristol will be using it for a couple of nights. Also, I need to tell them I'd like to be in Norwich for an early breakfast, much easier then to get easily parked. She could have a look around the farm. Even in the dark, the milking sheds are quite exciting. Will she need to be home at a certain time for her supper?"

Jane shook her head. "I've not had a moment to think about it. I'll give you a ring later."

"Don't bother!" said Nick. "I'll tell them there will be two extras for tea. They'll be all too happy to feed us both even though I had said I wouldn't be there this evening. Gran always cooks far too much. Gran thinks I'm too thin. I beg her to let me sort myself out but she won't have it. Just make sure you get something yourself."

Gran welcomed Emily with open arms. In next to no time, Emily was telling them all about the Christmas play at school and how she was the narrator. Casserole lamb followed by apple crumble disappeared into Emily as fast as she could chatter. Gran was overjoyed and even Gramps was amused. It was nearly nine o'clock before they were ready for home. Nick had no idea where she lived but a phone call and directions from Emily soon sorted that. He felt totally drained by then and reluctantly resisted Jane's invitation for a coffee, guessing that she and her husband did not want a visitor at that time of the evening. She too was tired having spent two, not one extra hour in the office.

Chapter 15
The Snowstorm

The light snowfall promised by the weather station was proving to be anything but light especially as the workload was busier by the day after the long Christmas and New Year celebrations. Nick was very grateful not to have the long drive from the farm each morning and evening. Despite every effort, it was proving impossible to get a long-term locum or even a prospective partner on the horizon. Penny had really left them in a hole. Retired local doctors were willing to fill in surgery time but not visits nor the coordination of the pharmacist, paramedic, nursing and other colleagues in the practice. Nick had found some Norwegian folding snow and ice guards for his tyres; so much better than the chains he had been using. They just clipped on and off. He was much in demand to do the outlying visits.

Mid-afternoon, Henry, the paramedic could not get his car moved from the carpark at the surgery. Having spent the morning with an ambulance crew, he had left his car in the surgery car park knowing he was working there in the afternoon. It was almost buried in the snow. Snow had fallen all day unnoticed by those inside. An urgent call had come in from the police. They had been called to a farm some four miles away from where a ten-year-old boy was missing after he'd stolen a tractor for a joy ride. They couldn't get a free ambulance or paramedic to the place and they were waiting for the dogs to help find the boy. Please could their paramedic get there soonest? Nick fully dressed by now in waterproofs and boots applied his snow guards and with some difficulty backed out into the road. The snow was still falling thick and fast making driving even more difficult. He knew the farm and knew the ill-tempered owner. There was a single police car in front. Henry followed Nick around to the back door.

On opening it and letting in a thick fall of new snow, they heard shouting. The farmer was almost screaming at another boy, yelling, "Where is he, damn you, which field, you bloody thieves." Meanwhile, he was shaking the lad.

Nick saw red. "Lay off, you idiot. Shut up and sit down. Get your hands off him. Now!"

The farmer turned around and was about to attack Nick. Henry, a burly fellow, intervened fending him off. The farmer raised his fists. "Who the hell are you? Get out there and start looking. It's my son who's missing. You're not wanted in here. Ginger."

"Calm down, stupid," shouted Nick. "Let's find out where to look." He turned his attention to the boy. "Now, stop blubbering and take me out to where it all started. I know you're wet and cold but until you say something, we, nor the police when they come, can start." Only then did he notice the farmer had a pair of crutches. No wonder he was frantic. He also remembered he hadn't told him who they were. "Sorry, Paramedic and GP!" he shouted as they left.

The boy led them out to a partly covered barn about 100 metres away. When out of the snow, he pointed miserably to

114

an empty area. "Well," said Nick, "is that where the tractor was?" The boy sniffed, swallowed and nodded. The space was small. It was a small tractor. "Come on, wake up," Nick continued irritably. "Which way did you go?" The boy pointed. "How long were you out?"

"Dunno." The boy sniffed.

"An hour?" The boy nodded. Just then there was a sound of voices and dogs barking. Also, huge flashlights. They congregated in the comparative shelter of the barn. Nick was able to give them a bit of an idea of direction. The police dogs and owners were given their orders and departed in different directions. Meanwhile, Nick, indicating to the remaining police officer to stay quiet, questioned the boy again. "Look, whoever you are, I was brought up on a farm and pinched the odd tractor to see if I could drive it. Did you turn it over?" The lad nodded again, now shivering in the cold. "Was it the biggest tractor?" The head shook rapidly. "Did your friend cry out? For help?"

The boy nodded. "Yeh. My cousin. Couldn't move. Ran for help. His dad can't walk and his ma's out. Came back and couldn't find 'im." He heaved convulsively and shrugged. The constable, who had been relaying it all, put an arm around the boy and guided him indoors.

Nick and Henry plodded slowly after the dogs. Henry explained the ambulances and paramedics were so overstretched he just hoped an ambulance would be there when and if it was needed. So many people who had fallen and broken bones were filling the A and E in the hospitals. Their torch lights were not nearly as useful as the police ones. Neither were they as fit. "Look," said Nick, "before we give up and leave it to the experts, an overturned tractor, however small, should show up even in this snow." As in all untidy farms, there was a fair amount of large discarded machinery around, any of which, covered in snow, could look like an overturned tractor. Foot and paw treads were rapidly being covered by the snow and now the wind was increasing. Perhaps the boys had not gotten all that far. He thought the 'hour' was far from correct. Probably the lad had lost all sense of time in his panic. At their very young age, Nick thought, any vehicle would have got out of control quickly. Especially in this weather. There seemed to be fences and obstructions in all directions and only one path where the boy had pointed. The dogs had fanned out from that point.

Henry was carrying quite a heavy backpack slowing him down. Nick offered to take over for a bit. Henry was watching his mobile for news. Suddenly he fell flat on his face cursing whatever was left in his way. To stop Nick from doing the same, he started pushing the snow away. "Hey, Nick, stop. Quick help." Nick pushed forwards, put the backpack on the ground and with snow still falling thickly, looked to see what the problem was, hoping and praying Henry had not come to harm. By a miracle, he had fallen over the child. As fast as possible, they dug him out with their hands. Henry proceeded to start pumping his chest begging Nick to unwrap his pack to find the foil wrapping. Nick grabbed the mobile to get the police back and as much help as possible. It was all taking too much time. It seemed impossible he could be alive in that cold and wet.

In reality, the help came so quickly. The lad was brought into the farmhouse and another even more urgent call went out for an ambulance. The police stayed long enough to ensure all was in order, leaving the constable to be with the father, and the mother when she returned from her shopping. Henry and Nick alternated with artificial respiration for nearly 40 minutes until another paramedic arrived, and eventually an ambulance. Nick thought there was a faint pulse. Henry was less sure. He was a chubby ten-year-old, looking very still and very angelic. No wonder father was in a mess. He watched the whole procedure in silence. Henry travelled to the hospital with the lad. Nick stayed long enough to talk to Mother and extract the full story from the other boy. It was distressing in the extreme, as Nick could hold out little hope of recovery to the father.

The nub of the story, when it came out, was the boys were bored. The 13-year-old tried for fun to start the tractor, pretending to the younger one he knew how to drive it. Ten-year-old climbed on board. The tractor started and with a little help, moved forwards, then backwards. Once out of the shed in the open, they were in the snowstorm, and neither boy knew what to do. A push on the wrong button lurched the tractor forwards, eventually, after a couple of 100 metres it hit something and turned over. The older boy was thrown some distance and took a long while to collect himself and find his way back. He had no idea at what point the younger one had fallen off. Mercifully, his parents collected him in silence before Nick left. He would not have liked leaving a 13-year-old at the mercy of that particular father.

Nick was rather surprised to hear nothing from Henry that evening but in a way guessed paramedics saw a great many more similar accidents than he ever would. Farm machinery held and holds a huge burden of suicides, fatal accidents and non-fatal serious accidents every year, never seeming to lessen despite endless publicity and safety devices.

Next morning at coffee break, Henry came over to Nick, grinning. "You're not going to believe this. I've just come back from the hospital after delivering a youngster to A and E with a broken arm. Young Pip, or whatever he calls himself is sitting up in bed, out of ITU and full of his fat self, probably the fat that saved him; must be good for something. Hope Dad is relieved, not cross or he'll soon not be feeling so full of himself."

Jane came across. "I couldn't help overhearing that. What happened?" Henry gave a succinct account of the event. She nodded sagely. "I wouldn't feel too sorry for him if I were you," she said flatly. "He's Emily's great friend of the moment. Spoilt brat, if you'll believe me. He comes back with her on occasions. I guess his rudeness and demanding is no different at home. His dad lost a leg umpteen years ago but manages to run the farm mostly just with his wife. Emily's been there a couple of times and comes home full of chocolates and sweets. He'll be fine and now even more full of himself."

Henry looked at her wryly. "Not exactly your favourite child, one gathers."

Jane retorted. "Oh, don't get me wrong. I think he'll be fine. A very bright lad."

The winter seemed to drag on longer than usual. The snow itself didn't last all that long but the slush, sleet and rain seemed never-ending. Nick was beginning to feel a desperate need for a break but could see little possibility of getting one. There was mud everywhere. On the roads from the sugar beet lorries, on the garden paths and most of all on the farms. The Easter weekend at least would give him four lovely free days. There was complete silence as to Penny's whereabouts but he was sure the MacAulay's would have contacted him if anything had gone seriously wrong. Adverts were now finding some applicants for the vacancy but none yet had looked good enough to follow up. Also, some of the regular locums were planning spring holidays making the workload heavier than ever. Maria confided Yuri was less well. She was not as cheery as usual, and often so late one of the others took on her first couple of patients. This was a blow as Maria was always stable, happy and willing to shoulder others' problems. Admittedly, Suzanne helped by agreeing to work an extra day a week. Chandra had decided to take another six months of maternity leave. And all the time, underlying his thoughts, was Jane. He needed to discover her husband, if she had one.

Chapter 16
Nick Plays in Rock Pools

Good Friday was sunny. Nick had a service he had promised to play for in the morning. Afterwards, rather reluctantly, he made his way back to the farm. Feeling particularly in need of something to do, he could not feel any motivation to do so. Saturday, however, dawned bright and sunny. Nick threw off his despondent mood, debated whether to visit Yuri or to drive to West Runton and walk to Cromer for lunch. One of his childhood favourites. He decided on the latter. It was still early but the parking area at the top of the cliff was already nearly full. The wind was chilly and Nick was glad he had brought his anorak. Heading off towards Cromer, he enviously watched the families playing on the beach. Many were actually paddling in what could only be a freezingly cold sea. As always, there were one or two diehard swimmers. The tide was on the way out and many youngsters were exploring the rock pools. As a child, they had been one of his great joys. He was tempted to do likewise but thought he might look a bit silly. Suddenly his daydreams were interrupted by screams of "Nick, Nick…" It took him some time to locate the source, then he saw Emily rushing towards him. With a huge grin, he held out his arms and Emily leapt into them giving him a massive hug. Excitedly, she grabbed his hand and dragged him to a nearby rock pool. "Come and have a look, Nick, come and see what I've found." Within minutes, he was doing exactly what he was itching to do. He noticed Emily run towards another family from time to time. He was turning over rocks and finding crabs, starfish and just about every creature there was to find in that part of the coast. Emily was ecstatic about every find. Dressed only in T-shirt, shorts and with bare feet, she appeared inured to the cold. Fully dressed, Nick was not. Standing up, he declared he must get on with his walk as he needed to warm up a bit.

Looking along the beach, first scanning it quickly and then slowly he could see no sign of Jane. He went back to Emily. "Where've you left Mummy?"

She replied, very unconcerned, "Oh, no, I didn't come with her. I came with the Bentons. They wanted to go home as Pip got wet and cold. He really can be a misery. I didn't and when I saw you, I said you would take me home later." For a moment she looked a bit apprehensive. "You will, won't you?" The cheek of it stunned Nick for a long minute. What incredibly irresponsible people! They had no idea who he was. Seeing Nick look so surprised, she said anxiously, "You do know them. They knew who you were. You must remember Pip; he turned the tractor over and nearly died?"

So much for his walk. Seeing suddenly the funny side, he'd done exactly what he wanted to, reliving his childhood rock pooling. Now he must pay for it. "Of course, I will," he said responded cheerily, "but you're jolly well going to have to stop for an ice cream at the café up there, even if we have to queue for hours. I never go to the seaside without an ice cream. Better find your clothes first." He pulled out his mobile phone and rang Jane. No reply so he left a text message. Then rang her again. She answered rather irritably. Briefly, Nick explained what had happened. There was silence for a while, then an explosion.

"How dare they do that? You might have been just anybody. Pip asked if Emily could spend Saturday with him. It looks like I'll have to give this afternoon a miss. I've had to come out of rehearsal to answer the phone."

Nick's answer came quickly. "Look, calm down, I agree they should never ever have done it but I'm at a loose end and will love entertaining her. What sort of time will you be back?"

There was a big sigh on the other end. "Look, forget it, I'll be back in under an hour and take over. I could shoot them." She shut the phone down abruptly.

Nick immediately returned the call. "Now, you look here!" Nick was annoyed. "I offered to have her, and genuinely want to do so. Go back, get on with your rehearsal. OK?" This time it was he who shut the phone abruptly. He gave Emily a little grin. "No good Mum coming back now. She won't know where we are." Emily clutched his hand and laughed. Over a fish and chip lunch in Cromer, he asked what her afternoon plans were, or what she would really like to do. Emily gave him a long thoughtful look.

After a while, she said in a small voice, "Can I really, really ask what I would really, really like to do?"

Nick looked back into the brown eyes that were looking at him so appealingly. "Try me," he said, wondering what on earth was coming, just hoping it was something possible.

She continued in the small voice, "What I would really, really like to do, is to go and hear Mummy sing."

Nick gave her the broadest possible smile. "Bingo! So would I! Hurry up and finish your drink while I make a few investigations and phone calls." 3pm St John Passion. St Peter Mancroft. No booking needed. It would be a rush and with the dreaded parking he hoped they wouldn't be late.

Nick was suddenly apprehensive as they queued to get in. "Emily," he said quietly, "this is a very grown-up, serious piece of music, do you realise that?"

She nodded vigorously. "I've heard Mummy practice it over and over again. I nearly know it."

"OK." Nick shook his head. "But if you get tired, or bored, let me know by a nudge and we'll go. Agreed?" The only seats available by the time they reached the head of the queue were ones at the far edge of the front row. Right in front of the alto section.

With his height and red hair, Jane had spotted them very quickly but apart from a startled look, made no acknowledgement. Nick didn't need to be worried. Emily sat absorbed in the whole thing, mostly staring at her mother. Jane popped out in the interval to give Emily a hug. She looked at Nick, in a bemused way. "Did you expect to be here this afternoon?" she enquired.

He nodded. "Normally, I would have done. I was having a bit of an overwork misery day and had planned to walk to Cromer from West Runton and back. On the way I was accosted by this young lady. We've had a wonderful time together, rock pooling, eating ice creams and a high-calorie lunch. This is Emily's choice. Entirely. She's loved hearing you practise and was keen to hear it all." At the end, Nick had a job prising Emily out of her seat. He knew how she felt. Music did that for him too.

Jane hurried over to them. "Nick, I don't know how to thank you but I do. Come on young lady, it's time for home, or shall we find a cup of tea first? I'm jolly thirsty."

Over tea and scones, they tried to discuss the performance with a very noisy party next to them. When Jane took Emily off to return in her car, Nick felt hopelessly deflated. The earlier part of the day had been such a joy. One big bit of him had hoped she would have invited him back.

Chapter 17
Accusation

The Easter weekend may have been unusually sunny but the bank holiday Monday evening turned to torrential rain and wind. It had not stopped since.

The reception area was awash with dirty wet shoes traipsing in and out.

Usually, Nick walked around to the staff door but it was just that bit further away and he had, as ever, not stopped to grab his waterproofs.

He was accosted almost immediately by a fully rain-coated figure with wet hair and a big smile. She had been in the queue for reception. "Hello, Dr Nick." As Nick looked completely puzzled, she giggled. "You don't recognise me do yer? Wanted an appointment to see yer 'cos I'm 'ere for me aunt. I 'as to see a right sticky old geyser where I live now."

Light dawned. Nick took her arm and ushered her through the door. "Carol, come, sit down and tell me about it all. I didn't recognise you." Not surprising. Her cancer treatment had not made her look at all unwell. Gone were the Goth attire and makeup. She was still slim but no longer skeletal. Her face looked really healthy. Carol giggled again as she complied.

"Now," said Nick briskly, "much as I'd like to spend time with you, I do have a long list of patients to see. Fill me in as quickly as you can. You look good."

"Moved in with me mum, see, and she feeds me fit to bust. Can't smoke there and 'ave to go outside. Not in this weather. Miss it. Finished me chemo and me radio. Kid looks great. Loves 'er school. Been told it'll come back but OK for now. Thought I'd just tell yer. It was only you could 'ave made me do it. Just, 'er...er...wanted to say, thanks." With that, she jumped up, planted a kiss on his cheek and left. Nick opened his door to find Maria standing there.

Maria had raised an eyebrow. "What on earth was that all about? You look thoroughly, well, embarrassed."

"I am," Nick replied as stonily as he could. "Patients don't normally leave by planting a huge kiss on my cheek."

Maria roared. "What a way to start the day! She was only in there for two minutes. Wow, lucky you!" This only caused Nick to turn an even brighter red. "Really came to see if you'd like a meal this evening, not to shock you but to give Yuri a bit of company. He's finding this weather very depressing."

"Not surprised. I think we all do. After the miserable winter months and Easter and all that. Yes, thanks, I'd love to." Secretly, he hoped Yuri had at long last, made some progress in finding some paternal relatives.

Nick's last patient left. He heaved a big sigh. It had been a long and difficult day but now he was much looking forward to his evening with the Skowrons. The door opened. Jane hurried in without her usual gentle double knock. "Nick, there are two large policemen waiting for you. I've managed to hold them back until the last patient left but they're on their way in now."

Without any preamble, they entered, filling the whole room with their presence. "Now, lassie, if you'll excuse us," he said turning to Jane, "the sergeant and me 'ould like a word with this gentleman, please." Jane backed out slowly looking very worried. Nick pulled out a second chair.

With just a frisson of impending disaster, he suggested, "Would you like to take a seat? Then we can discuss whatever you have come for?"

"No sir," the constable said steadily, "we'd prefer to stay standing if it's all the same to you." They both were all of Nick's height but much burlier in build. Their faces were expressionless. Nick looked from one to the other in puzzlement. "We've got a warrant for your arrest for assault and we'd like it if you would come quietly to the station in our car. If you walk quietly out, we might not disturb any patients still in the building." He read out the well-known warning about anything he might say being used in evidence. Nick's jaw had dropped and for a long while, he couldn't think what to say. The policemen looked doggedly at him, awaiting a response.

"What on earth am I supposed to have done? It can only be a mistake," he pleaded.

The sergeant nodded. "Mm, they all say that. Best you come with us, sir, and we'll discuss it at the station. Meanwhile, do you need to tell anyone where we're going, and if you've got the name of your solicitor handy, you might find that useful too. Perhaps ring your Union?" For a few moments, Nick thought he was going to lose his temper but reined himself in time to remember it would be counterproductive; much better to go along with it all and sort it out later. He was shaking, part anger and part with fear of the unknown.

The half-hour journey to the police station was accomplished in silence, apart from the continuity of the police radio. Nick could not think of a single thing to have prompted the arrest. At least they had not handcuffed him so could not have expected him to be violent. On arrival, he had been checked for weapons and his iPhone and contents of his pockets removed from him. Then, and then only, was the full charge read out to him. He was accused of sexual assault on a woman patient. Carol had brought the matter to the police. A serious charge. Enough to have him struck off the medical register very quickly. Certainly, suspended from that very moment. Nick was so shocked and taken aback he could not think of a single sound to make. He gave a throaty whisper, "But that's crazy," he stuttered, "Carol! It's daft. I didn't…"

"Now, now," said the sergeant stonily, "just save all that for the courts." Nevertheless, the constable wrote it all down, word for word.

A wave of terror overcame Nick as he waited. Crime and detective TV were not something he would choose to watch but Gran adored them, so he was not entirely unfamiliar with the procedure. He was escorted to a dismal interview room. Grey, made even more dismal with a low-powered light bulb, needed as the high window was facing another wall. A different and very young-looking policeman now sat with him. He was inscrutable with eyes everywhere, except making contact with Nick. Nick was left with nothing but a turmoil of jumbled, frightening thoughts.

Eventually, after what felt like hours but must have been much less, a middle-aged lady came and sat opposite him.

Smartly dressed in a light grey suit and floral blouse, she also stood nearly as tall as Nick. Her grey-streaked dark hair hung to her shoulders in a neat bob. Her voice was melodious and sounded educated. "Good evening, Dr Grovenor, I'm Detective Chief Inspector Smith-Bonn. Before we start, would you like a tea?"

"Could it be a coffee?" asked Nick in a very husky voice. He'd need some sort of liquid if he had to answer questions. She turned to the constable. He nodded and left the room. She waited for his return. More silence. The coffee was placed in front of him alongside a glass of water. The coffee was exactly how he did not like it. Weak, white and sweet.

"Now, would you mind if I turned on the recorder?" Nick shook his head. It would be all the same if he did object. She spoke irritably. "You'll have to say yes or no. The recorder cannot see you shaking your head."

"Yes." Nick hoped his voice would be stronger if he had to answer questions. He gulped at the tasteless coffee. She proceeded to name the four of them in the room and to accept Nick's denial of the need for a solicitor this evening. If this went on, he'd need to get one of the Medical Defence Union ones.

"Carol Green states you came into the reception area of your practice surgery where she was waiting in a queue to make an appointment. You recognised her, took her by the arm, marched her along the corridor to your consulting room. She thought you would be attending to her needs as a patient. She was very surprised to get such quick treatment but had no idea of your real attentions. After a very short consultation, you then leant forwards, grabbed her remaining breast and kissed her very sexually on the lips. She managed to struggle free and fled from the room. A woman was waiting outside and could witness her frightened retreat from your room. She also thinks it would be easy to find others who were waiting in the reception area who could witness your taking her by the arm and leading her out of the room."

She held up her hand to stop Nick from speaking. "You don't have to say anything but anything you say will be used by the investigators. You might prefer to wait for your solicitor before you say anything."

Nick saw only too clearly he was not in a position to defend himself, so sat quietly, trying to disguise his trembling hands, trying to work out exactly what to say. He could see the constable poised with pen and notebook. Eventually, he collected himself. "I am totally innocent. It's nonsense. Firstly, Carol was no longer a patient of the practice. I could in no way offer her any investigation or treatment. Some months ago she moved back in with her mother to a different area. She was not Carol Green when she left our practice but I cannot remember what it was then. She could only ever have expected to exchange a few words with me. She could not have made an appointment to do so online, which she would need to do. Secondly, I was fully booked and no receptionist would have allowed her to have those few words with me today." He was speaking increasingly fast, stumbling over his words. "Thirdly, it was only by chance I came in that way. It was raining hard and a good bit further to the staff door. Carol was extremely sick when I first saw her way back in August. I was so delighted to see her happy and well at that chance meeting, I invited her to fill me in very briefly on her treatment. Yes, I did take her arm to move her out of the queue. With hindsight, I can see that was unwise." Wearily,

Nick shrugged his shoulders. "I doubt she was in my room for more than two minutes. She told me all was well and how the kid was enjoying school and about her treatment. For no reason at all, she suddenly jumped up, kissed me on the cheek and rushed out of the room giggling. I relayed the incident to Dr Skowron who was waiting for me to finish just outside the door and we laughed. Oh, hell, I can't believe this is happening." He fell forwards resting his head on his hands.

DCI Smith-Bonn spoke. "Terminating this interview. The accused is in obvious distress."

Nick forced himself upright. "You're right. I'll get onto the Defence Union for a solicitor. It's a nightmare. I can't believe she could do anything like it. It's not the straight, girl I got to know in the autumn. She wouldn't have trumped up something like this. Can I go now? Get a taxi or something. I haven't eaten."

"Not such a hurry, you'll need to come before the magistrate. We'll need bail, if the magistrates feel it is safe before releasing you. The desk sergeant will sort that out. You will need to remain in custody overnight, Dr Grovenor. PC Andrews, please get some sandwiches out of the machine for the doctor."

It was after midnight before Nick could finally put his head on the hard pillow in the cell allocated to him. He had sent texts to everyone who needed to know. Tomorrow, he would somehow have to tell the grandparents. Even in the worst moments at the so-called community home, he had never felt so utterly wretched. He could see the headlines in the Eastern Daily Press very clearly. All the trust he had built up with his patients now destroyed, his partners would never trust him again and his poor, poor grandparents. Sleep did not come. Even if his innocence was proved, nothing would be the same again.

Chapter 18
Nick Finds a Family Tree

Nick was feeling lower than he had ever felt as he tried to tell the Solicitor, sent to him by the Medical Defence Union, the whole story. To start with, he felt grubby, his clothes in a mess, he was desperately tired and he didn't take to the man appointed to help. He got the impression the solicitor had just assumed him to be guilty. However, he did as he was told, gave the magistrate his details and pleaded 'Not guilty'. Bail was granted, and eventually, he was released to await an appearance at the Crown Court. To his surprise, Charles was in the court waiting to drive him home. Charles put his arm around Nick. "It's OK lad. We know it's a put-up job. All of us, including the staff, from manager to cleaner, are with you. We'll do everything in our power to help. Now, shall I drive you back to your grandparents to tell them about it and get some hugs? When you've had a couple of night's sleep, sorted out the General Medical council and found an MDU lawyer you like, we'll discuss work." Nick nodded miserably. He was now as near to tears as could be. He hadn't expected understanding from anyone. An unattached young doctor was bound to be presumed guilty by newspaper standards.

The next few days passed in a haze of interviews, suspension from practice and financial arrangements. Two trips to London. His grandparents were amazing. They knew him so well; knew his ethics and absolutely knew he was the victim. Every day someone from the practice came to visit, carrying gifts of chocolates and cards of support from patients and staff. Best of all was a letter from Sir Edward, this time addressed to 'Nick' offering his sincere support knowing him to be entirely innocent. Nick was overwhelmed by it all. So many patients had written to say how good he had been to them, the women stating his behaviour was always impeccable. There were even a couple of young girls who wrote saying they would have loved it to have been them! He now had a lady solicitor who collected facts and gave no hint she didn't believe him. She must be near retirement but all of her very short grey hair, her five foot nothing exuded competence. She asked him to bring her all the cards and letters of support he had received. Maria would have to give evidence anyway but hoped to represent the practice.

Nick tried to think of ways he could find another job if he was no longer allowed to practise medicine. Medicine was his life. Perhaps he could go into research? He spent many of the empty days exploring what in the world he would be able to do. Perhaps he should study for a post-grad degree in Biochemistry? Once his favourite study subject. At least it would be three years of getting away from everything. But, oh, how he would miss seeing patients so much.

He hadn't made the front page of the EDP but there was a sizable heading on page two which left no doubt about his guilt. Fortunately, they had not picked up on the fact he went to church and played the organ. All the sort of meat an ever

ever-hungry press would have loved. In the editorial and correspondence columns, the following day, were many accounts and stories of perverted doctors.

Maria had asked him if he could spend some with Yuri. Yuri, himself had asked if he would. Nick was worried about facing yet another person after the terrible accusation. Possibly, if there was any news about the other side of his family, it might divert him a little. He said yes, he would go.

It was a lovely early summer day and Yuri met him at the door on his arrival. "It is a good day, eh Nikolaus? The sun, it shines, the daffodils shine and you have come to see me, good?" Nick smiled reached down and took both of Yuri's hands in his. He was a little shocked to see how much Yuri had deteriorated. It made him feel guilty he had not made the effort to visit him earlier. The winter months must have been so tedious. As if he could read Nick's mind, Yuri continued, "And yes, you notice I am less well? Maria sees me daily so does not notice. I need to visit home, my home in Poland before it is too late. I have to tell her. But now, Nikolaus, you are in trouble. It will pass in days or years, I promise. Now, come with me." Despite the sunshine, it was cool outside and the warmth of the AGA welcome. The kitchen was the best place to be. The dog looked up as they came in, dropped his head and went back to sleep. "Nikolaus, it will be quicker if you make the coffee. Proper, not that powder. Ugh! That is not coffee. See! Beans, grinder, percolator and cups all at the ready." As they sat at the table, Yuri lifted the cover and displayed a plate of iced cupcakes. "The girls made these for you. You must eat!" Nick willingly complied, beginning to feel more relaxed. He ate two despite finding them very oversweet, sticky and a little tough. Yuri watched him. "Not good? Me, I do not eat cake. You must take some home." Yuri wheeled himself to a desk hidden in a corner, picked up a folder and brought it to the kitchen table. "However, Nikolaus, I do have a story to tell you. And I will tell it from the beginning. Are you comfortable, or do we move to the living room?" Nick shook his head. He was happy in the dream kitchen and there was at least one more cup of the excellent coffee in the pot. "Right! We begin. With you, Nikolaus. You were given a birth date. Helpful? Very roughly, 2000 registered each day. Half must be girls eh?" Nick nodded. "So, 1000 girls not needed. Eh?" His heart was thumping and for the first time since his arrest his attention was captured. "27 were called 'Nicholas'. Not many eh? From the medical school entrants register for your parents year she was 'Mary Grovenor'. He was James Elvedon. Not difficult. Charles volunteered his name from a photo of the whole year. Now, when people change their names by deed poll, they are not original. No! They keep the first name or sometimes the first letter but they change their end name. Yes, again keeping the same initial. Your father did. He was no different. He became Ellsmore. Which should have been yours too!" Nick looked at him in surprise. This aspect had never really bothered or even occurred to him once he could use Grovenor and have a real family name. He shook his head. He was perfectly happy with Grovenor. "Yes, yes, Nikolaus you could have been Dr Ellsmore, not Dr Grovenor." Nick smiled, for the first time in an age, a genuine smile. He got up to pour more coffee and accidentally picked up another cupcake. "Ugh! Ugh! Nikolaus, you will be sick. Now we continue? Yes? But first, I need to know it is Ellsmore. So, I go to deaths. Your mother died soon after your birth, or why would she leave you in an orphanage? Or perhaps she died and he did? So, I search the deaths for a month beginning with the 'E's for all lady deaths aged 21 to 23. Only one fitted. Died." He wagged a finger at Nick. "Certified as 'Post-partum infection, secondly, by drug abuse'. Here, here I have her death certificate." He laid it on the table in front of Nick. For the first time, Nick became aware of the pile of papers in the folder in front of Yuri. "You were just six days old. Terrible. Terrible. Now, to find your father's death. We have a name, an age and easy. You were eight months old! He was junkie. But for the first ten days of your life someone cared. You were well fed on delivery to orphanage, and content. So, I search. His medical school entry says he went to a St Joseph's school in Islington. So, it is not boarding, so he lived in Islington. The electoral rolls are kept. But the year their son went to medical school there is no entry on the electoral roll for the couple, I am by now sure are his parents. I find his birth certificate. Here. They most definitely are his parents. They must have moved from Islington when their son went to medical school. I then chat to the registrar at their medical school. I had to chat with her a lot. I made her laugh. She then said to ring me back. She does. There is a letter from a Jim Elved on from an Essex address to ask for an address for his son. A sad letter. They know their son is very sick; they want to find him. It is filed. It gives their actual address in Essex! We find them. Only eleven miles from the orphanage. You see, Nick, you did have other grandparents. We all have. And they have names. Jim and Elsie. Now I try being very professional. James took you from London to his parents in Essex. He dies as I said some months later. But why do his parents not care for you? But they take you to the orphanage, all anonymous. No details. Perhaps they are busy? Perhaps they could not love you? No! I search again. Only Jim is on the next electoral roll. I find. Elsie died of cancer when you were just two. I guess she was too ill. Jim, he could not cope." Yet another piece of paper landed on Nick's pile. "Jim married again two years later."

Nick could not wait any longer. He asked agitatedly, "And is he still alive now?"

Yuri shook his head slowly from side to side. "No. Very sad. Both got killed in a car crash soon after marriage. I am trying to find a newspaper account of the accident. My last task."

Nick relaxed back into his chair and signed deeply. "So, even if I'd done something about finding them a few years ago, it would have been too late already."

Yuri replied quietly, "It always is. We all leave things too late. I think you may have a great uncle somewhere but he would be nearly 90 so I do not search for him. There, Nikolaus, I leave you my invoice. And the papers. And now, we have some lunch. It is all at the bottom of the AGA. All we need otherwise is the bread and the butter. Real butter, not the dreadful as good as ones. They're not butter. Ugh." The thick chicken and vegetable soup was delicious.

Ikbal phoned or face-timed Nick most days. The practice was badly overstretched without Nick and Penny. As yet, they had not found a new partner in place of Penny. Although no formal notification of her resignation, Charles agreed they could now assume she had separated herself from the practice leaving them free to advertise for her replacement. A number of excellent retired GPs were plugging some of the gaps but the remaining partners were still far too busy. An advertisement in the British Medical Journal now had at last resulted in a number of replies. Ikbal suggested Nick should come to the surgery about 5ish when he hoped to be finished for the day, to help go through them.

"You do realise, Ikbal," Nick said seriously, once they were seated in Ikbal's room at the surgery, "it is a very possible outcome I shall never work as a GP again? Should I really be taking any part in this exercise?"

Ikbal banged on the desk. "Oh, don't be so utterly ridiculous, Nick, of course you will!" He looked at Nick irritably. "At the very, very unlikely, worst you will only be suspended for a short time, then you will apply to be reinstated. A couple of years at most. Then you may have to have a chaperone but not worse. And of course, we won't let you go. So, let's look through these. 11 applicants. OK?"

Not really convinced, Nick decided he had to take an interest. "Three are absolute rubbish but I don't think we need to interview more than three anyway. Best have a fourth in reserve in case one drops out before the interview. Of the three 'rubbish' ones, one was 63 years old, another had previously lost his driving licence and been suspended for drunk driving, and the other had four previous practises on his CV in just 15 years. The 'why' was not obvious. It will take each of us a couple of hours to whittle them down to just four. Charles, Maria and the part-timers will need to make their choices as well from the remaining seven."

Both Ikbal and Nick agreed substantially after studying the seven CVs. There was one particular lady applicant who lived locally and seemed to tick all the boxes.

Chapter 19
Jane Has a Secret

Nick's mobile rang just before eight in the morning. He was fumbling through the newspaper trying to find the crossword. His heart was racing, fearing that such an early phone call could only mean one thing, bad news. It raced even faster when he saw who it was. "Hey Jane, what can I do for you at this hour in the morning?" he asked breathlessly.

She answered immediately. "Nick, I wonder if you would do me a very, very big favour? I had forgotten to put the school teacher training day into my diary. Emily forgot it too but once remembered was hoping to have a lovely free day while the teachers did their thing. Since the beginning of April, Emily has harassed me daily to ask you to fulfil your promise, to arrange a farm to visit. Your grandfather had offered to show her the new lambs and calves once they arrived. I don't know if you have any. If you have, please could we pop to see them very quickly and then I would arrange with your grandfather to see them properly another day. I do need to get into work as early as possible." She sounded so harassed he was more than delighted to help out.

By now, Nick's heart was beating at a slower speed. "Oh great, just bring her along. We have lambs just about everywhere and I think a calf was born in the night."

In no time at all, Emily came dancing into the kitchen, followed closely by Jane. Nick grabbed Emily's hand and took her out to where grandfather was waiting for her. Gramps happily took over her conducted tour.

Nick hurried back to tell Jane he had nothing to do all day and would look after Emily. Instead, when he returned to the kitchen, he found Jane wrapped up in Emma's arms. What on earth had happened and why weren't they his arms? He had never, ever, felt such yearning before. Totally bewildered, he tried to take in the tableau. "What…what's happened?" he pleaded. "Has something just happened or did you know each other already. Do you?" He saw Jane was sobbing her heart out. He could barely stop himself from rushing to take her into his arms.

Emma answered him very quietly, looking over Jane's head, which was now buried in her shoulder. "Yes, we met around nine or ten years ago and in very tragic circumstances. We have not met since. This…this is quite a reunion."

Nick sat down in his chair and waited impatiently for what seemed an eternity. "Are you going to tell me where or what this is all about? Or is it something you would you rather I didn't know?"

Emma drew away a little from Jane and asked, "Jane, shall I tell Nick what this is all about? Or is it rather something you might not wish him to know?"

Jane pulled away from Emma, grabbing a couple of pieces of kitchen roll and drying her face. She took a few deep breaths, shook her head and swallowed hard. "No, I don't mind Nick knowing about this. He will understand it is something I prefer not to talk about but it all came back so vividly when I saw you. Nick, I cannot believe this is your grandmother. It is wonderful but…but I think I shall start crying again if I have to relate the story. Please, Emma, may I call you Emma? I must go and find Emily and get to work. I keep on hearing my mobile ping."

As Jane was about to run away, Emma grabbed her arm. "Now just you listen to me; Emily is obviously enjoying whatever Tom is showing her. You go and get on with your work and come back at teatime and enjoy a meal with us." Jane opened her mouth to protest, looked from Nick to Emma and decided they meant it. It would, when she thought, be such a relief not to have to pop in on her all day at the surgery. She could really get on faster, and no school either, would give her a further couple of hours in which to catch up. Teatime, she guessed would be around six o'clock. She nodded and left.

"Gran, I'm desperately anxious to hear what happened but I'd better first go and see if Emily is alright." She was. He found her in among the lambs, sitting on a straw bale with a bottle of milk held very correctly, so the lamb wouldn't be swallowing air. It was a very small lamb.

"Nick, Nick," she exclaimed, excitedly pointing to the next pen, "this mummy sheep had three lambs four days ago and hasn't got enough milk to feed them all, so I'm helping. When she's drunk it all, I am going to lift her up and put her back."

Nick grinned at her. "You just might find her a bit heavy you know. They weigh a lot more than they look."

She nodded. "That's exactly what Gramps said but Barry will be free when he's finished lambing in the next shed. Then we're going to go and clear up two more pens to make room for some more expectant sheep. Oh, the bottle's empty. She's drunk all of it! Could you help me?" Nick pulled back the gate, stepped in. He watched her try to lift the lamb, which now flopping dangerously in her arms, her rueful smile giving him the opportunity to help. Emily was about to take to her heels and to next barn and find Barry.

Nick asked quickly grabbing her arm, "Hey, just a minute, Em, who gave you permission to call my grandfather 'Gramps'?"

Emily stamped her foot. "He did. And my name is Emily, not Em!" With that, she was gone. For a full quarter of an hour, Nick forgot all his troubles.

Back in the kitchen, Emma was drinking her usual mid-morning hot chocolate, looking very thoughtful. Nick sat down, rather apprehensively, opposite her. She got up, took the percolator off the AGA, putting it and a blue Wedgewood mug in front of him. "Nick, I don't know enough of the background to tell you a lot about Jane. I met her only once on what must have been the most terrible day in her life. Gramps and I went to a service in a village whose name I've forgotten, somewhere near North Walsham. We'd never been there before, and have never been back. Our curate had finished his training with our church. He was a right nice young man. He invited us to hear his first sermon in his new parish. We sat fairly near the back of the church, which really were quite full. Just in front of us was this very pregnant girl. She exchanged greetings with us but was preoccupied with looking at the door, waiting, she said, for her husband. At the end of the sermon, a police constable, who must have come in right quiet like, rushed forward, asking loudly if anyone knew anything about a car number. It were Jane who leapt to her feet and struggled past the three people next to her." Here Emma stopped and drank more of her chocolate. Nick's coffee had gone cold. She was finding the telling distressing. "I took one look at the terror on her face, then, as no one else moved to help, pushed past my neighbours to go out with her. The policeman looked frighteningly serious, said nothing but opened the doors to let us into his car. Less than a quarter a mile away were a car almost halfway up a tree. Her husband had now been put on a stretcher, covered over. There were a fire-engine and lots of police cars. I didn't rightly know what to do. I reckoned I shouldn't be there but there weren't no one else. I don't know what happened next but she flung herself at me screaming 'it's him' over and over again. All I could do was hold her tight and wait. Police kept asking questions but I had no idea even who she were Emma stopped, put her head in her hands and tears were falling down he face. Nick said nothing, knowing she would continue in her own good time. It must have been a horrible sight. Emma gave a sigh. "In time, she calmed down enough to give them her name and hand address. She managed to get out her parent's address and asked to go there. She were still hanging on to me for grim death. Didn't mean that. But I didn't know what to do until she were some place safe. So I went in with her. The policeman told them what had happened but she were still hanging on to me like. So I tried to explain. Lovely couple. Looked so shocked. Made tea before asking more. Then her ma said, quiet like, 'do you reckon he were still so angry about the money he didn't pay proper attention to driving?' And

Jane had replied, she'd tried reasoning with him but it was getting late, so went on to church first, expecting him to calm down and follow her." Emma shrugged. "That's all I know. If Jane wants you to know more, she'll tell you. I guess she is terrified someone will say too much and Emily will find out. Can't see a car crash needs to be a secret. Must be more."

Nick ached for her. Having guessed a little of how Jane would have thought, he believed she blamed herself for the argument, whatever it was. He now understood why she was so calm, distancing herself from people. He remembered the magic hour when she and Emily had come to his flat for coffee and ice cream. She fitted exactly and was so relaxed and he had felt he could discuss all sorts of things. He knew it was when he had fallen hopelessly in love with her. Not the violent emotional fall in love but a serious, deep, quiet love overwhelming him. It was the real reason he had not followed up the music connection. And that performance along with Emily there. He had so wanted that day to go on and on but she so obviously had not. Rejection would be far, far too painful. But he had discovered she was a widow, and if only he waited, if he was cleared, he might be able to tell her how much he loved her. Penny had never made him feel anything remotely like this.

It could be too late already to declare himself, anyway, he might have to move when this awful cloud over him had resolved. If ever. Would it ever be possible to meet his ex-patients and friends again?

Chapter 20
Maria Requests

Nick was fixedly looking at his now cold coffee, his mind wandering, trying to plan a possible future. Hearing a commotion outside, he looked up seeing his cousin frantically chasing an errant sheep with a bleating lamb behind him. He had no inclination whatsoever to go and help. In fact, he felt a total lack of inclination to do anything. Dimly, he was aware of a knocking on the back door. Emma was over at the main farm helping his cousin's wife with lunch for half a dozen hungry farm workers.

Unwillingly, Nick went slowly to answer the door. He was just in time to see Maria disappear down the path. He rushed after her, catching her seconds before she got into her car. "So sorry, Maria," he said breathlessly, "I was having rather a bad morning and couldn't be bothered to answer the door. Do come in and I'll make you a fresh coffee."

She replaced the car keys in her pocket and turned around. "Also, partly my fault," she said a little wryly. "I was trying to pluck up the courage to ask you a big, big favour and nearly chickened out when the door wasn't answered."

This woke Nick up. "Surprise me. I need a cry for help. I feel utterly useless. Am I to have a chance to look after the girls? I'd love that."

"No…no, though there are times I could do with it." She followed him into the kitchen and sat down facing him. He got up, moved the remains of his breakfast plate and mug to the sink, placed a couple of fresh mugs on the table and set the percolator working. Maria shook her head slowly. "No. It's Yuri. He is deteriorating now. He desperately wants to visit his parents and brothers in Krakow before it is too late. Before the Covid-19 pandemic, we went every two years. What with the surgery premises move, and doctor shortage, I fear it could be too late for him if he had to wait for the practice to be up and running, and well, could manage without me for a couple of weeks." She fell silent and looked expectantly at Nick. He could not imagine how in any way this could affect him. After a pause, she went on, "I…I just wondered if you would take him instead of me. I cannot leave the practice just now. No, no, please do not batter yourself anymore but you know the situation." All sorts of thoughts ran through Nick's head. Why had this happened to him? He was far more use working, and then letting Maria accompany Yuri. He was on bail and they held his passport. He wouldn't be allowed to or would he? He could see, and almost feel how intensely needy this was for Maria. She watched all these emotions flash across his face. He had been staring at the table. Suddenly he got up and poured the coffee. She took it black as he did.

"Yes, Of course I will take him. If allowed. I've never even thought of going to Poland. It will be an adventure. Something I can really do to help."

"Yes," she said eventually. "I see with great relief you do not reject the idea. For me, for Yuri and for the practice it would be good. I do have a couple of police contacts, and a magistrate is a good friend of mine. I have made enquiries. Your bail money is substantial. They will just want to know where you are, I think."

Nick actually smiled. "At last, something I can do! I'd love to, if it can be done. I might feel a member of the human race again, for a while. I do enjoy Yuri's company. I'm sure he is aware of his deterioration but multiple sclerosis can be very fickle. He might well get there another time with you. I gather the immunotherapy helped for a while. There are new things in the pipeline too. Also, for me, it's a long way to September and the Crown Court."

Much to Nick's amazement, they treated him pleasantly at the police station. After his previous experience there, he was more than a little apprehensive. Arrangements had been made, presumably by Maria, so a few signatures later, he with passport, made his way to tell Yuri.

"Come, come Nikolaus. We drink good coffee and I tell you what we do." It was a sunny, cloudless day. Nick, now familiar with their percolator, made them both coffees. Yuri wheeled himself into the conservatory amongst the many plants. He was lying back with his eyes closed enjoying the warmth. With nothing else to do, Nick also made himself comfortable in one of the deep wicker chairs. He closed his eyes, relaxed and waited for his coffee to cool. The silence was so peaceful. Eventually, Yuri roused broke the silence. "Nikolaus, Nikolaus," he said excitedly, almost childishly, "for the next three weeks you forget your problems, eh? You will be busy, and then, hey, we come back. Your name is cleared and you can start work again. Eh?"

Nick made a face and answered ruefully, "I wish!"

Yuri continued dismissively, "But maybe it takes a little longer but we go. You will go sightseeing every day. I tell you where to go each day. I visit my parents and my three brothers. You will meet them all. My brothers, they speak a little English. My parents, no. But you and I, we stay at the Balthazar Hotel where it is very comfortable and they know me. My brothers, they take holiday so we can spend time together. They deliver you to your tourist day. One brother has a big enough car to take my wheelchair. Not this one, you understand but my folding one. Not comfortable but necessary." Nick nodded his head a few times. Eventually, Nick managed to break into Yuri's excited commentary. Yuri's speech was slow and slurred. Nick felt any interruption was hurtful.

"But, can we get reservations at such short notice?" he asked, slightly bewildered at the speed things were happening. Yuri had pre-empted and made plane reservations already. Travel and hotel already booked.

"And," – Yuri's face lit up – "Krakow is so, so beautiful. There is so much to see. The marketplace! The biggest and best in Europe. In the world! And, when you've finished looking at that, there is another marketplace underneath. There is. Yes, it is so, so medieval. The whole city is medieval. And you climb to the top and see the view. Ah! You will enjoy. And I, I will spend time with my parents and my brothers."

Back home, he had a bounce in his step. Something to do. Something to look forward to. Emma breathed a sigh of relief.

She and Tom had been increasingly worried to see the effect the false accusation was having on him. They knew it to be false but also knew Nick still had a lot of unresolved issues from his childhood. The nightmares were much less frequent but they still happened. Noisy enough to wake them. They were pleasantly surprised when he changed ready to go out to the farm to help with the lambing. Today she'd brought lunch over from the farm, and while enjoying the excellent casserole, he regaled her with the morning's happenings. Afterwards, he disappeared into the lambing sheds to help Brian and the others at the height of the season. He returned, covered in farm muck well after Tom and Emma had finished their tea meal, looking healthily tired. He rushed in, ran up the stairs and had a shower then came down looking clean and cheerful. Tom and Emma looked at each other in relief. He tucked into the re-hearted meal with gusto. The first time since that awful evening he had really looked hungry. "I've offered to do the night shift for Barry tomorrow," Nick said brightly. "Brian is done in at the moment and needs a night's sleep. Don't worry, Gramps! I haven't forgotten all you taught me. Obstetrics for humans is not all that different. They still have ones that come out backwards and ones that get stuck and ones with placenta problems. In a way, sheep are easier. For one thing, they don't call you names, you can get a hand in and get on with turning and untangling them and then you can leave it to them. Well, most of the time. I'll be fine. The Texels are just about due and Brian is bringing them in tomorrow. Can't think why anyone has them, need more intervention than all the others put together."

Tom jumped in. "Ah, Nick lad, what you should know is how good the meat is. Best of all, the hotels love them and pay good prices, and don't they just look bootiful? Those broad faces, the tight wool and the thick meaty rump?" Tom was quite excited. Nick laughed.

Chapter 21
A Day in Norwich

Saturday morning and Nick was having a day off. The lambing was slowing down and he was needed less and less. To his great surprise and delight, just as he was clearing the table from breakfast, Jane and Emily walked straight in after a perfunctory knock on the back door. "Have you come to see the lambs again, Emily? Or to what do we owe the honour of your visit here today?" He daren't look at Jane. He was afraid his face would give him away.

Emily giggled. "No. I'm not. Though I expect I'll go and look. And I want to see that calf who was new. But I'm here to help Grans with the cooking. We're going to make meat pies and rhubarb ones. It's all arranged."

"Well, well," exclaimed Nick. Surprised yet again by the familiarity of the 'Grans'. "But no one told me you were coming. So important and no one told me!"

This time it was Jane who intervened. "I gather you've been busy," Jane said in her calm quiet voice, "but also suggested to Emma it might be better to not give you too much time to think. I need to go into Norwich this morning to see Robin's solicitor. There are still some difficulties that even after all this time have remained unsorted. Mostly, I have to add, due to my inertia." Nick nodded; he could empathise with that. "And I need to shop. The dress shops here are so lovely but more than my budget allows. I like M and S. Does both of us well. And, here is where you come in. There is a recital of Vaughn-Williams Sea Symphony at St Peter Mancroft later and I wondered if you might like to join me there?"

Nick's mouth dropped open. He couldn't believe it. One of his most loved pieces. "Would I? Gosh, yes I would." And with Jane. A whole two hours of her company!

"Well," Jane went on, "you can either try to park on a Saturday afternoon, use the Park and Ride, or you could come in with me now when there's usually a chance to park. You'll need to do your own thing in the morning; we could then meet up for lunch. And go from there." Nick took absolutely no time to consider. More than anything he wanted to be with Jane. Close to her. Also, he genuinely did new things for Poland. He wasn't going to miss a moment of her company.

"Give me five minutes." With that, he disappeared up the stairs, put on a jacket, collected his wallet and found a pair of fairly clean shoes. Emily had disappeared long before Jane had finished. She had discovered the chickens at the side of the house and was busy with Emma replenishing their water and feeding them. "Your car or mine?" asked Nick.

Jane considered for a moment. "Yours, if you wouldn't mind. Mine is getting a little geriatric and occasionally gives up. Never quite sure how it passes its MOT. Can't work out how I'm ever going to afford an electric car when they become compulsory."

Having decided the Park and Ride would save them a slow journey into the city, with the uncertainty of where to park, they were fortunate in securing a place not a half-mile walk to the bus. The holiday season was just beginning to get busy with extra coaches and cars. On the way, conversation was easy, discussing music, the practice and the fate of some of his patients. Jane went off to the solicitor. Nick made straight for Marks and Spencer. It was a long while since he had stocked up on clothing, a new toilet bag and above all, a suitcase. Feeling rather cluttered by his purchases, he stuffed them into his new suitcase and decided to explore St Peter Mancroft church itself; a huge perpendicular church right in the marketplace. It was one he had seen from the outside on his childhood visits to the city but never taken time to explore. Last time he had been so preoccupied looking after Emily and watching Jane, he had barely noticed his surroundings. Its history of performing music was legendary. He stood back for a moment as he entered. The vast ceiling and the impact of lightness was surprising. For the next hour, he was absorbed in the medieval history and some even going back as far as the Normans. Gun powdered by the Puritans in the seventeenth century, he was staggered by the craftsmanship exhibited when a few years later all the shattered beautiful glass had been reassembled into what was now the east window. He surveyed the organ loft with its spiral staircase. Nick reckoned one would need a good head for heights to climb into that organ loft.

He met up as arranged with Jane laden with shopping. Much of it he managed to cram into his suitcase. He noticed she kept looking at her watch as they queued for a table. "Why the hurry?" queried Nick.

"Oh, just that we have a rehearsal at 2:30 and I would like to get something to eat first."

"Rehearsal!" exclaimed Nick. "Of course, you have! I'd forgotten that." For a moment, his heart plummeted.

"Mm," replied Jane nonchalantly, "didn't I tell you? Our director is very knowledgeable and very strict. We are all auditioned before we join. Nerve-wracking, I can tell you." With that, there were a couple of tables free and the queue was allowed to move. The noise in the restaurant stopped all but the most necessary conversation. They were glad to get out, fed, if not particularly well. He debated with himself how to occupy the afternoon. Parking a car in the city itself meant there would have been somewhere to put the shopping. He decided he would go to watch the rehearsal. After all, how could one possibly get enough of music? Jane was delighted. "I'm so glad you're coming to that. You'll see how he conducts and his scathing remarks of which we take no notice. I'll take the suitcase into our cloakroom which only leaves you with a couple of my bags."

Later, seated in a good position to hear and see the choir, he watched as they all filed in, well drilled to find their seats. It took him a few minutes to locate Jane in the second row of altos. He did not take his eyes away from her. He could not get enough. The music and numerous interruptions made no difference; there was only one person in that choir. He was still sitting there, mesmerised after it all finished. He was thrilled when Jane came out to find him. "Nick, we're all having tea and cake. There's someone I want you to meet. Come with me." Nick's heart collapsed. Had she already found another soulmate? He couldn't bear that. With relief, he was pulled through the throng of singers to be introduced to a late middle-aged, severe-looking man, abnormally thin and with a balding almost shaven grey hair. His face softened as Jane approached.

"So this is Nick," he said, transferring his gaze through his horn-rimmed spectacles to Nick, "I gather, young man, you're an aspiring organist, who might be looking for lessons?" The voice was clipped.

Taken aback, Nick replied hesitantly, "Yes...yes, I do try and play each Sunday for a church, when I can but I have a long way to go before describing myself as an organist."

"There is a scheme here where someone dedicated can go on a three-year funded course of lessons. We had appointed our three places for this year but one little chap has got an unexpected scholarship to Eton's sixth form. I ought to hear you play first but I know Jane well, and she wouldn't countenance asking me to see someone not able to reach a competent standard."

Nick was silent while all the problems he had raced before him. "It seems to be too good to be true," he said eventually. "When...when does it begin?"

"Oh, not until September but if you'd like a couple of lessons first, I can do that privately?" Coming September, he and his problems must have been resolved in some way. Yes, he would do it. And, he'd arrange a lesson first. He'd have to ask Jane for this man's name as he hadn't been introduced.

Nick's face lit up. "I...I would love that."

"Give me a ring. We'll arrange it." With that, he strode off.

Jane turned to Nick with a smile. "I've known Richard for a large number of years. Long before I lost Robin. He was a great friend of Robin's father which is how I summoned up the courage to join the choir. He is the organist here. There are several assistant organists too. He is pure gold and so is his wife." So, Richard was just a friend. He could relax.

Nick did his best to get immersed in the music as the performance got under way. After all, it was music he knew but he found yet again all his thoughts were wandering and his gaze came back to Jane. Before he went to Poland, he resolved, he would get himself to a psychologist and get himself sorted. He couldn't do or say anything to Jane before that. He had massive hang-ups and issues he had never been able to face. Images of Penny flashed into his mind. She had found every opportunity she could to get him into bed with her, using all her powers of seduction. Involuntarily, he shook his head. He had drawn back on the brink knowing he would face the humiliation of failing at the last moment. His student day attempts had ended in disaster. It would matter now.

Chapter 22
Up to Heaven and Down to Hell

Helping Yuri into the taxi made Nick realise he had taken on a big task. The overnight stay at the hotel at Heathrow had been a learning curve. Yuri was a natural early riser so there was no problem him getting up in time. For the first time, Nick appreciated they were to travel business class when the assistance member of staff led them into the lounge. With more than a five-hour journey ahead of them, he was grateful. Shortly afterwards, they were joined by an elderly man in a wheelchair. Evidently, he was Polish and within minutes, Nick was left to his own thoughts while an animated, incomprehensible conversation took place beside him. Using the internet, Nick had attempted to learn a few basic words of Polish but not enough to hold a conversation. His thoughts, inevitably, went back to Jane. For some reason, he had never asked Maria the name of that psychologist. Often he had been on the brink of doing so. It could only be fear of what it would reveal. How else could he not do something so important?

His reverie was broken when the assistant reappeared to take them through passport control, search and all the other paraphernalia of modern airports. Nick enjoyed the priority treatment. Yuri was moved out of his wheelchair into a pushchair and elevated on a lift into the plane and moved into a seat. It seemed a long while before any others boarded but Yuri was given a Polish newspaper by an air hostess that had been left on a previous flight. Nick had bought an English one for himself earlier, so the time went quickly. After a tedious but comfortable flight, the process was reversed. More delay as they were the very last passengers off the plane. As he was being placed back in his chair, Yuri spoke urgently, "O, Nikolaus, I forgot to tell you, only Maria calls me Yuri. My name is really Jakub. My brothers, they call me Jakub." Now comfortable in his own wheelchair, they emerged to find Yuri's brother Borys awaiting them with his enormous car. Borys was the image of a younger, fitter Yuri. To the day he left, Nick never was sure which brother was which. Had he been fit, Yuri would have been another pea in the pod. Each day as he was escorted on various expeditions, Nick had to await a clue as to know his brother was escorting him.

The whole journey had been almost too much for Yuri. By mutual agreement, they drove straight to the hotel. The hotel was stunning, situated in the medieval part of the city. Worth a galaxy of stars, so unlike the well-known chain hotels. Yuri was greeted like a long-lost friend. Which he was. The manager had been at school and university with him. Royalty could not have been made more welcome. The two-bedded room even boasted two bathrooms and access for the disabled. Not good access but Nick reckoned Yuri would cope. Coffee and cake appeared and the three of them gratefully relaxed. Invited to have a snack, Nick accepted but Yuri decided to rest in bed. He was soon asleep. After unpacking his new suitcase, Nick went for a short walk to stretch his legs.

For the next nine days, Nick was escorted by one of the brothers on daily excursions but first, he was invited to meet Yuri's parents. Interestingly, to Nick, they lived on the fourth floor in one of the hundreds of massive Communist built blocks. Father was an elderly likeness of the boys, Mother prematurely aged for a reason Nick couldn't determine. Both bestowed many smiles on Nick. He returned them as best he could but it was no substitute for a proper conversation. Lots of translating by Yuri, which was very funny at times, ending with them all roaring with laughter. The room was very crowded and Nick was glad when Alex decided it was time to go.

He visited the huge and wonderful outdoor marketplace, the underground one found by the archaeologists with its museum, the Wieliczka salt mines, the city hall, St Mary's Basilica with the climb and view from the top, the Wawel castle, and an unnerving visit to the Auschwitz-Birkenau site. All so wonderful to see but stilted exchange of all Nick wanted to see and ask was far from the same as having a kindred spirit. If only he had Jane with him. Perhaps one day he would come back with her. If only.

By day five, Nick was beginning to get tourist overload and begged a quiet day without more stimulation. It was such an incredibly rich city. He would return and take it in slowly. Sitting quietly in their room, Nick attempted to catch up on texts and emails. Ikbal, Maria and Charles had either phoned or emailed every day since he had been suspended. Today there was one from Charles that literally made him leap out of his chair. His hand was shaking so much he could not hit the right button for the surgery. The text from Charles had simply said, "See you back at your desk on Monday." Nick paced around the room. What? Why? How? When he did eventually hit the right phone number for Charles, it was engaged. He tried again. It was still engaged.

In the end, he rang Jane. She answered immediately. "Hello, Nick," sounding unusually reserved, "Isn't it wonderful news."

Nick could hardly get the words out. "I don't know! Is it really true? What's happened and why?"

"It's OK, Nick," she replied gently, still sounding rather strangely distant. "No need to panic. We don't know any details but on the front of the EDP is an article saying Carol admits it was a set-up job and the article goes on to say 'she tearfully hopes you will forgive her'. That's all we know. There is an official 'private only' letter to you, which with your permission I will open. If it exonerates you, I will copy and send where relevant."

Nick had not recognised how different Jane sounded from her usual self. "Please, like now! I'm so excited I can hardly bear to stay here."

Jane sounded almost uninterested. "Only a few days. Celebrate with Yuri." Then she added casually, like an unimportant postscript. "Oh, and by the way, I've handed in my notice. I'm due two weeks leave and will be gone before you get back." No goodbye, just that. She had hung up immediately. So final. In the stunned moment he took to take this in, he knew it was no good ringing back. It then registered how coldly she had sounded all the time he had been so excited. He froze. The bottom fell out of his world. This was far more important than the wonderful news of his possible reinstatement. Impulsively, he texted on her private line. 'I love you, Jane. I love you with all my being. I can't take this in. I love you more than anything.' And he blamed himself angrily for being so utterly crazy not to have declared himself before. He wanted to be there, to take her in his arms and hold her. Then she might have known how very much in love with her he was. He stopped suddenly and thought. Why did she put the phone down so quickly? Was it because she had known he was in love with her? And she could not return that love? How much more natural to tell him why she was going and where she was going. Or by any miracle, could she be in love with him, and needed to move away, believing he couldn't return it? Or did she think the gremlins that haunted him would make any relationship impossible? She knew about these. By the evening, having missed out on lunch and tea, he had collected himself enough to relate to Yuri the good news. "There!" said Yuri with a huge grin. "Did I not tell you it would all be resolved?"

Nick replied wryly, "You must have known something I didn't then! I'd even tried to plan a new career for myself. So thankful I don't need to. However, did you have a good day?"

Yuri gave a very tired nod. "Very. But I shall now not be sorry to get home again. I miss my girls, the two little and the one big. My brothers and above all my parents miss seeing them too. But not to be this year. Another, perhaps. Nikolaus, I am tired tonight. We eat well, my brothers and I. Tonight, you go down to dinner alone with your book. Eh? I retire early. They bring me a small snack. Tomorrow we celebrate."

Later, having showered, changed, partaken of an excellent meal that he had barely noticed, Nick found himself a quiet corner in which to drink his coffee and make a few phone calls. Firstly, he phoned his grandparents, ostensibly to say hurrah, how good it was he could get back to the surgery but really to find out if Emma had any idea where Jane was. They were so full of the good news he got no response whatever from the latter request. Next call was to Charles, who too, was bubbling with the good news. "Nick, that's absolutely great. It will be so good to have you back. Every member of staff is smiling. Oh, I didn't tell you. Jane has decided to up and move."

Nick couldn't hold back. "But why, Charles, she seemed so happy and settled. I can't…I can't imagine the place without her."

Charles replied prosaically, seemingly having no idea how important it was for him. "I'm not surprised in some ways. She did a heroic job moving the premises with not a single hitch. Also, she now has the place running like clockwork. She is really bright and needs to be challenged. I haven't done anything about replacing her yet. We'll wait until you're back and up and running." Nick shut his phone down miserably.

Next call was Maria. "Hello Nick, you're early this evening. Everything alright? Isn't it wonderful news? We're all bubbling. I now feel I can take Yuri and the family away for half term. I do need a break." She was only vaguely interested in Jane leaving. "Oh, Nick, has anyone told you we've appointed that lady doctor we all liked? She's agreed to come and starting in September, so we're going to have to muddle through the summer." Nick sat with his head in his hands for some time, pulled himself together, realising he could do nothing until back in the UK. He must not, above all, dampen Yuri's time in his beloved Poland.

Returning to Mersham, Nick found it difficult to join in all the celebrations of his reinstatement. Everywhere he went his hand was shaken or he was subjected to hugs. He welcomed it all but was, underneath really desperate to find Jane. Tom and Emma were grinning from ear to ear. Totally unlike their normal abstinence, they had bought a bottle of Prosecco with which to celebrate. After the special meal, he asked as casually as he could, "Gramps, has Emily been here while I've been away? I guess she'll have wanted to see the calf and how the lambs have grown."

Tom, looking a little embarrassed answered, "Oh. Ar...I reckon hers been here a couple of times. Great little lass, that. Real sad they're moving."

Nick tried to sound nonchalant. "Any idea where to?"

This time Emma chipped in quickly before Tom could continue. "She didn't rightly know last week but she'd got her eye on a couple of places south of Norwich. Said she'd come over when she could. No more." Somehow Nick didn't quite believe her. Her lips closed tightly and she looked away from him. He knew he would get nowhere by pushing.

It was well into the afternoon of the Friday before Nick was given time to think of a plan. Firstly, get to the school by 3:30. He was a wee bit late but could see children of her age just beginning to come out. No sign of her. He had driven Emily home a few times. It was not all that far, so that was his next stop. There was no 'For Sale' notice which puzzled him. He had driven past the house and arrived just to see the removals van leaving. Too late to ask where it was going. No sign of Jane's car anywhere. He guessed she must have gone first. She hadn't. During his time away in Poland, she had purchased a second-hand KA of more recent vintage than the one he knew. Jane and Emily had watched from their bare front room window as Nick's car drove around and around.

Both were crying. They were leaving everything they wanted behind for the second time. Now, at a total loss as to where to go next, Nick decided to go the flat. His flat looked very neglected after his absence. He made himself spend the evening energetically putting it back to the usual shipshape way he liked it. He sat down at the piano but could find no inclination to play. Decided to play scales and arpeggios and all the dull things he usually avoided. After a while he gave up. Daylight had almost gone and it had started to rain. In a sort of desperation, Nick put on a pair of running shoes. He spent the next hour on a hard run, returning in the dark so exhausted he could only manage a quick shower before swallowing a glass of water and getting his head down.

The next morning, just as he was about to leave for his usual weekend at the farm, there was a call from Maria. She sounded very distressed. "Nick, I need your help. I am feeling desperate or I wouldn't ask. Yuri is really ill this morning. Charles has just been. He's got pneumonia and, and I've promised to have Emily for the day while Jane moves and it's Saturday and I can't cope." There was a huge gulp on the other end.

Without thinking, Nick replied immediately, "Of course, I can have all three girls for the day. I'll come and collect them right now. I'm really sorry, Maria, I've grown to love Yuri so much. I hate to think of him being ill." All the time he was speaking he was thinking of Emily. If he had Emily for the day, Jane would be fetching her and he would see her. Of course, he would have her for the day and the other two. He'd ring Grans now. She would love to help.

An hour later, Emily, looking very important, was giving Sophia and Tanya a conducted tour of the farm. With minimal supervision from Nick, this took up most of the morning. With a lunch of soup and sandwiches, Emma had somehow discovered they were to be there for tea as well. Nick was full of anticipation. Every time he imagined Jane coming to collect Emily, his heart raced. He would see her! He would be able to tell her how much he loved her. He would insist he took the girls back in the evening. Then he couldn't miss her.

Emma happily organised cooking for the girls in the afternoon, preparing tea and making a supply of cakes. Sophia and Tanya had been more quiet than usual when they had arrived. Gradually, with so much to see and do, they had become their usual excitable selves.

Over tea, all Nick's hopeful dreams fell apart. Sophia and Tanya were arguing about which room Emily was to sleep in that night. Would he dare to ask Maria outright for a mobile number or an address? That would be unkind at the moment. Could he ask Emily for hers? He was pretty sure anyway Emily did not have a mobile phone. Should he offer to have the girls on the Sunday? It would be very difficult. He had a service to play for and he would not like to ask Emma or Tom to give up their church attendance. Every way he tried to find Jane, the way was blocked. It was now increasingly obvious she didn't want to meet him. If only he knew why he might be able to get some part of his life together. Did she really not love him? He couldn't believe that. Why wouldn't she at least tell him why?

Chapter 23
A Worse Story

After another couple of restless nights, Nick was no wiser. Find Jane, he must. As he was brooding, his phone rang. With difficulty, he collected himself enough to accept Ikbal's call. "Nick, we must celebrate. Are you free tonight for me to take you out for a good meal and a real chat? We can catch up on practice news. And our own."

Nick brightened up. If anyone knew anything about Jane, it would be Ikbal. They had got on so well. "What a lovely idea, Ikbal. I'd love to come. What about Parva?"

"Don't worry, Nick," he replied with a chuckle, "I've asked her permission first!"

Having seen the pile of correspondence on his desk, Nick decided to spend the morning re-orientating. Just as he left, the flat two older teenagers walked towards him. One said, as she pointed at Nick, "That's him!" The other one hissed at him. "It's scum like you should be in prison, not the poor kid you abused." It was so utterly unexpected he was stunned for a moment. They had almost walked past him when his anger at the injustice overcame his common sense. He yelled at the one who had called him scum, causing her to turn around and face him. He continued furiously, "If I hear that once more, it will be you in trouble with the police. That poor kid was a set-up. I have no problem taking you to the police now!"

"And I'll have you for assault. Shouting like that is nothing short of assault," she screamed.

This brought a small group of onlookers. An elderly gentleman of very military appearance intervened. "Having problems, Dr Grovenor?"

Nick gradually calmed down. "Yes, I am," he said decisively. "I've been completely innocent of any crime but these girls called me scum. It made me see red and wonder how many others see it that way." He looked around but both the girls and the small crowd had dispersed.

The gentleman nodded sagely. "I'm afraid there always will be the ones who claim there is never smoke without fire. You'll have to get used to it. It'll go in due course. People come and go and they forget." He smiled. "But don't go as far as grabbing arms. You nearly did. That really is assault."

Nick drew in his breath. "Thank you so much." Feeling subdued Nick continued, "May I ask who you are? You sound very authoritative."

"That is my job, young man. Among a few other things, I was in on the Penny affair and saw and heard how good you are." Nick looked surprised. With that, whoever he was, strode onwards.

Later he and Ikbal were sitting opposite each other in a nook in a popular Greek restaurant on the Cromer Road. It was early, and there were few other diners. "Nick, we need to get our exchanges in before it gets full. Then it's far too noisy but you'll enjoy it. How's it all going?" Nick related the incident of the morning. Ikbal nodded sagely. "I guess I understand that sort of thing. I get it all the time."

Nick grimaced. "Then I guess I'll just have to put up with it."

"Let's hope it's not for too long then, for you. We have now put a notice up in the waiting area, just above where patients book in, to offer a chaperone for any consultation if required." Nick put his hands over his face. Ikbal went on, ignoring Nick's discomfiture, "You may find one or two ask but probably most will accept your innocence as right."

After hesitating for moment, he asked tentatively, "Why did Jane leave in such a hurry?" An unwanted flush spread slowly over his face, obvious, even in the dim lighting. At that moment, some fat olives, garlic bread and dolmades appeared with glasses of water, along with the menu for the evening. Instead of answering, Ikbal immediately started going through the menu. After much discussion, both decided to have the mushrooms stuffed with haloumi cheese for starters. Ikbal chose the vegetarian spanakopita and Nick the lamb kleftiko for their main courses. While waiting, they decided ouzo was the correct drink for their nibbles and after that the pineapple juice.

"Do you realise, Nick, this is the first time in over six months we have been alone together for a chat? Usually we've both, I think" – here he raised his eyebrows – "have been enjoying Parva and the children's chat?"

Nick nodded. "Hugely!" he responded. "I've almost felt part of the family on occasions."

Ikbal continued, "I promised to tell you the story of how I came to Postams. Interested?"

Nick suddenly really did feel interested. "Wow! Yes, I am! Somehow there's never been enough space for it." The restaurant was getting noisy. Their starters arrived. It was a little while before their conversation was renewed.

"You, I know, had a difficult start in life. In a very different way, so did I. I'm the afterthought in a family of six. My father was an active Hindu lawyer fighting persecution. I was born in Tharparker in Pakistan. Not a good place for us Hindus to be. I gather father was in a movement working so all faiths could live together in peace. Before I was old enough to understand, my older brothers had already finished their university days in India. My father disappeared from my life when I was about five. To this day, I have no idea what happened. There were a number of Hindu boys at school and I really didn't feel persecuted. My mother qualified as a doctor in Mumbai but with six of us, never got around to practising again. When Father disappeared, she had to work. Why she didn't take us to Mumbai with her, I have no idea. So far from home. I was left in the care of my one remaining sister. She can only have been 16, if that, and was waiting her chance for an education somewhere. Suddenly, when I was 12, an unknown uncle appeared from New Delhi." He paused. "Oh, here are our mains. Don't they look amazing?" Nick gulped down the last of his ouzo and gave his glass to the waiter.

A Greek band was just starting up. It was going to be hard to hear the rest of the story but first, he must enjoy the meal. Nick's lamb was the most succulent and tasty imaginable. He savoured every mouthful much to Ikbal's amusement. But Ikbal, too seemed to be enjoying his as much. The band was now in full swing with singing and everyone clapping to the rhythms. It was impossible not to join in. "Don't worry, Nick, let's join in the fun. We can sit here until midnight and drink coffee or what you fancy." The birthday boy in a big party was toasted by all the diners. Later when the band stopped for their break, Ikbal, encouraged by Nick, continued his story. "This uncle, who could have been anybody, demanded we, my sister and I, packed as little as possible and to be ready by dark. He was so fierce we obeyed. We were terrified. He barely said a word on all that long, long journey to Karachi airport in his hired car. I think we were both too frightened to sleep. We were hustled through various airport controls. He held brand new passports for us. New Delhi was a shock. So was the almost palatial house we were taken to. Our aunt was a miserable, frigid childless woman who did nothing to make us feel welcome." Nick could only try to imagine the huge parts of the narrative Ikbal had omitted. His own problems faded. Ikbal paused, seeing if Nick was following. Reassured, he continued.

"We were fed, clothed and entertained by a large army of servants. Our uncle, we discovered, was a wealthy banker, brother to our father. OK so far, Nick, or are you getting bored?"

Completely taken out of himself Nick shook his head vigorously. "Far from it. I'm totally enthralled. Oh, bother! No, I don't really mean that but here comes the band again. Please carry on and I'll try to hear you above the noise."

As Ikbal spoke, Nick had to get close as he could to hear him. Ikbal had obviously thought through and prepared his story. "It could only have been a week, or at the most ten days later, he sat down with just me and explained very tersely and briefly that he had at long last found which prison my father was in and made contact. Father was serving a 20-year sentence. If, he survived that long. My eldest brother was also

171

in prison somewhere and my next one was somewhere safe in India. My mother had moved to a different clinic in Mumbai. I was to go to England to be educated. The next day. I was given my false passport, a large sum of English money, a case pre-packed for school and put on a plane to Heathrow. I was too stunned to ask for an address for my mother or for anybody really. Even my uncle. The only contact with anyone in India since has terse emailed instructions from him. I followed the crowd to the exit and if I hadn't seen a placard with my name on it, I would have had no idea what to do. I was driven to Postams, housed for the night and well, the rest you know." He shrugged his shoulders and looked to Nick for a comment. That was so much worse than his own situation. He had grandparents. Here, in Mersham. For a long, long time, he sat staring at his empty coffee cup, oblivious of the noise around him.

"How you have coped with all that I can have no idea. You are the bravest person there exists. Torn from your family, and left with none. What on earth would have happened if Postams had not taken you? Did they know the situation?"

Ikbal sighed ruefully and shrugged his shoulders. "Probably but I've no idea. I had enough money to last for a long while."

Nick hesitated before going on, "Have you thought of asking Yuri to help find your relations? Don't you desperately want to?"

Ikbal smiled. "Of course, I have. Mother at least should have been traceable through their medical register but having no idea of her first name, not her age nor the year of her qualification, it's nearly impossible. I can't even work her details out as I have no idea how old my brothers are or were. We do have a very common surname. Yuri hasn't given up. No trace of any of my brothers but there is a record of my father who was discharged from prison five years ago."

Nick thought for a moment. "What about the sister you were left with? You knew a bit about her."

Ikbal shook his head. "Hopeless. That uncle and aunt would have had no compunctions about getting her married off, fast. I believe the aunt's name was of all things, Miranda but I have not a clue about his."

"What happened when you left Postams?" Nick asked.

Ikbal suddenly looked sad. "It was such a shock. The day after GCSEs. The head called me to say a car was coming for me at midday. An Indian family had been told to collect me, send me to a day school in London and were being paid for my board and lodging. They were not particularly friendly. Once at medical school, my bank account was topped up but I was on my own." Nick could think of nothing to say. All these years, he had been filled with his own miseries but here was someone much more deprived but generous, who had learned to live life fully. Perhaps it had much to do with his Hindu faith. Nick felt utterly humbled.

Chapter 24
Nick Finds Chrissy

Nick was now sure there was a conspiracy of silence surrounding Jane. Feeling fobbed off by everyone, he dared not ask outright. He would only flush and make himself look silly. He had tried every indirect method he could envisage. He blushed like a teenage schoolgirl when he even thought about her. He had tried texting, phoning, emailing, all to no avail. She had changed everything as far as he could determine before he came back from Poland. There had to be a reason, unimaginable to him, making it more painful. If she was in trouble, he wanted to be there. He had even tried to see if Emma could remember the church where she had first met Jane. Emma claimed to have no idea.

"Nick, are you frantic at the moment?" Charles poked his head out of his room.

"Not frantic," replied Nick, "just busy. Why?"

"Mrs Robinson in the nursing home has died, and they'd like a death certificate so they can get her body moved. It's a burial but in Winchester so there's a modicum of urgency. She was 101. I guess I'd label it multi-organ failure or old age. She was amazing until a couple of weeks ago. You saw her too when they first grew concerned about her. I think she was in the lounge then."

Nick nodded. "Yes, I do remember her. Actually, I have a visit in the same direction, so it'll be easy for me to go. I should be back by two." He collected up the necessary items and drove off along the coast road, enjoying the sunshine and scenery. Mrs Robinson was in a spacious attic room on the third floor of the nursing home with a wide view over a children's playground.

As he was watching the children playing, the Matron drew alongside him. "Those poor women and children. I spend the time I haven't got watching them. It's the back of the women's refuge in case you didn't know."

"No," Nick said thoughtfully. "I did know it was somewhere at the back here with a private entrance off the lane." Suddenly, Nick jerked to attention. No, it wasn't possible. He was imagining it. He focused on a woman with unkempt straggling hair and a red dress who was pushing a toddler on a swing while yelling something at an older child.

Matron stared at him. "Dr Grovenor, are you alright? You look as if you've seen a ghost. Do you need to sit down?"

"No, no. I just need to get closer to that woman pushing the child on the swing. If it's who I think it is, I have seen a ghost."

She took his arm and gently led him away. "This is about as close as you can get. The fence and railings stop views from the lower floors." By the time they arrived on the ground floor, Nick had recovered his composure. He covered the journey back to the surgery in record time. There was no Jane to go and ask for the phone number of the refuge but the new administrator, Sybil, was very efficient.

Sitting at his desk with trembling hands, Nick picked up the phone and dialled. It was answered immediately. "Anglesey House." Nick took almost too long in answering but after the second "Hullo," he managed to ask if he could speak to Mrs Parsons. "That's me," came the brisk reply. "How can I help?"

His words fell over themselves. "It's, it's Dr Grovenor here from the Mersham surgery. I was signing a death certificate in the nursing home when I saw in the playground someone who…who…just about saved my life many years ago. If you doubt my credentials shall I ring off and you can ring the surgery back?"

There was a short silence. "Carry on for the moment. I'll do just that if I'm unsure. No. No, I've a better idea. I have a tetanus jab due at 3:00 this afternoon. Can we fit it in around that?"

Nick drew a big breath. "Yes, that would be much easier. It's a long story. Her name is Christine, I presume, though she was always Chrissy to me. A…a skinny redhead called Nick back in Essex." With that, he put the phone down and found he was really shaking. If it really was Chrissy, he would need to see her soon. Wisely, he waited for Charles to be free to put him in the picture. As Nick was going out of the door, he said gently, "If you need putting together again afterwards, I'll be around."

Soon after two o'clock, Nick was called out on what sounded like an emergency. It rapidly brought him back into his working world. Having instructed reception to hang on to Mrs Palmer at any cost, he sped off in the Sheringham direction. An elderly man had fallen and his wife was worried. He was up on his feet again but she seemed very concerned still. As he drove into the short drive, straight off the main Cromer Road, the door opened and a diminutive, very elderly woman stood in the small porch. "I'm that worried!" She started speaking before Nick had got out of the car. "It's the third time he's done it. He goes down with a big…"

Nick came alongside her and gently took her arm. "Let's get inside, shall we?" he asked. "Then we'll have a proper talk."

She hustled him into the traditional rarely used front room with its faded brown settee and two armchairs on either side of the unused grate; three flying ducks over the mantlepiece and family photos on every available surface. She sat on the edge of a chair and invited Nick to sit opposite. Her cardigan was buttoned up incorrectly making one pale blue corner dip. Her straggly iron-grey hair looked unloved. Along with that and her constantly wringing hands, she was a picture of agitation. "It's like this," she continued, "the first time was about a week ago. I heard this crash in the kitchen and something break. There he was on the floor. He lay there and laughed at me. Said, like, he didn't know what had happened. Back up on his feet and clearing up the mess." She paused for breath. "Happened again after breakfast this morning. He was telling me something like, and there he was on the floor. I'd started dialling 999 but he got his self-up, shook his head and said to stop, he was alright. But it happened again just now and I wasn't going to take no to call a doctor this time. What you're going to do?"

"What we are going to do," said Nick steadily, "is to go and find your man and give him a once over. OK?"

As he got up, she shot to his feet. "Oh, no, please don't go in there. I haven't washed up yet."

Nick smiled down at her. "I wouldn't even notice if you had a week's washing up there! But I'd rather see him where he's comfortable." The living room was much cosier with a newspaper spread out on the table and a tall, thin man dressed in shirt and braces leaning over the table reading it. He looked a picture of health. His medical history barely existed. There was no record of any illness at all. Apart from vaccinations and an HGV medical, there was nothing.

"Sorry, lass has bothered you," he said as he removed his broken one-sided spectacles and went to stand up. "It's nothing. I trip or something but I can't think on what. I just fall. But I'm right as rain after a minute or two. Takes me a while now to get up off the floor, like!" Nick nodded. This was going to be difficult. The diagnosis was obvious from the story but persuading him he needed to do something about it was the problem. After a slow and careful cardiac examination, Nick put his stethoscope away and closed his bag. The patient grinned at Nick. "There, that was a waste of time, wasn't it?"

Nick paused and chose his words carefully. "You're right, young man. But." Here he waited until he had the man's full attention. "You need to be got to hospital today. Like now. In an ambulance."

The man roared with laughter. "Don't be so right daft! I'm not going to no hospital. You dies in them places. There be nowt wrong along with me."

Nick held his hand up. "Please, I'm not joking or playing games with you. I'm certain the electrics that keep your heart beating have gone off the rails. You may need a pacemaker to put it right. Have you heard about pacemakers?" For the first time, his patient looked puzzled. He nodded.

There was a gasp from his wife who covered her face with her hands and started wailing. "I told him there was something bad. He won't die, will he?"

Nick turned rapidly to face her. "Don't be silly! Of course not. He'll need a few days to get it sorted, and then he should last longer than the rest of us."

This had all taken longer than he intended and just prayed Mrs Palmer had waited for him.

She had, and was irritably tapping her hand on a briefcase in her lap. She got up immediately. Much younger than Nick had expected, somewhere between 30 and 35; shortish, slim with her fair hair cropped close to her head. She got up briskly as Nick walked through. Despite her air of efficiency, she was dressed casually in jeans and a loose pale blue T-shirt. He opened the door of his consulting room. Before he had time to sit, she was speaking. "Yes, I'm well aware you had an emergency but I must be brief. My deputy is on holiday and I'm not entirely happy with the lady in charge. Now" – she drew breath to continue – "before I get Christine on one side, I need to be absolutely sure of where we plan to go with this coming together of two people whose paths have obviously gone in two very different directions. Do you see what I mean?" Nick nodded. This was not how he had planned the interview. He felt like a naughty schoolboy in front of the headmaster. "I was sufficiently happy with your account of your time at the home together to believe you absolutely. But why do you wish to see her now? What can you hope for either of you to achieve by it? Don't you think it will upset her to be reminded of those days? Have you thought of that?"

Nick was silent for a minute, then spoke quietly, "Those of us who went through what we went through in those two years is never going to forget. I guess, like me, Chrissy still has nightmares and rarely gets to sleep without some frightening memory invading her mind." He looked up. Mrs Palmer seemed to relax a little. "I was scrawny, very small for my age, in with a gang stealing anything easy, rebellious and with a very short fuse. For two years, Chrissy protected me from myself. She never left me alone in the playground, she kept me away from the gang when she could and life would have been so unendurable without her, I would have run away. I'm all too aware I would have ended up with a life of crime alternating with periods in prison without Chrissy. Then I would never have found my wonderful grandparents. Do you begin to see why I so desperately want to help if I can?"

Mrs Palmer looked at him steadily with her piercing blue eyes. "Yes, I do," she said slowly. "And how do you think you can help? Not, I hope, by planning to be the next man in her life?"

Nick brought his fist down angrily on the desk. "No, no, no, of course not." He needed to get some control of the discussion. "That would be impossible. But I have thought carefully. My grandparents have a bungalow on the farm which is currently being vacated by the retiring stockman. The new one lives at home with his parents. It is just possible she might be able to use that while waiting for something more permanent. I've phoned my grandparents this lunchtime, and now need to give them time to think it over with my cousin who runs the farm."

Mrs Palmer was silent for a while, then spoke, carefully choosing her words. "Do you realise she has three young children? And an older fourth in foster care. It was her pregnancy that alerted officialdom to the abuse in the home."

180

Nick shuddered. "That brute got her as well? I thought he was mainly into boys." He covered his face in his shaking hands. She continued to survey him, now exuding real sympathy. Eventually, Nick spoke, "Where did she go?"

The answer was almost spat at him. "Back to Mother, just out of prison, in a one-bedroom high rise flat. The baby and the mother's new man arrived together, and she was asked to leave. Baby went into care and Christine was left on the streets. Every man she picked up with seemed to batter her. This latest nearly killed her and is in custody awaiting sentencing. She spent three weeks in hospital. Children and she are just recovering here. Now do you see why I'm protecting her?" The latter was said so viciously, Nick read into it that she too had her own experience of abuse.

Chapter 25
Searching

Nick was in a bit of a dilemma. He had a much-awaited organ lesson in Norwich on Saturday morning and had booked a concert in the evening. The choir in which Jane sang was taking part. Then, he might at the very least be able to feast his eyes on her, and maybe, even pluck up the courage to speak to her? Or, should he forgo the concert to get back to the farm for his usual overnight stay at weekends? He was very anxious to see if his grandparents and Barry had reached a decision about Chrissy.

His first organ lesson was not on the high up principal organ as he had hoped but on the one used for the church choir practices. His home taught pedal skills were analysed. Either you did the toe only, or you did the heel-toe. A book of exercises. Another on correct stops and names. Yet another on hand exercises. Nick came away exhausted. He decided to treat himself to a Loch Fyne fishery lunch.

The need to see Jane was overwhelming. The concert won. To occupy the afternoon, he decided it was time he visited the castle as an adult. There was an exhibition of wildlife. The whole thing was geared for children. Wandering around the castle, he was so preoccupied with thoughts of

Jane and worry about Chrissy; it was small wonder he took little interest in what he should be seeing.

Arriving early for the concert, he found a seat where he could clearly see the choir but was not too visible himself. Carroty hair was so difficult to hide! The very mixed programme looked interesting. Madrigals, Sea songs, opera choruses and flute solos. Difficult to see a theme but guessed there was one if only he could focus on the programme. Not a concert he would have chosen had it not been for Jane.

He came fully alert as the choir started to find their seats. He watched intently every single woman as she filed into her place. He scanned the alto section over and over again. No sign of Jane. The life went out of him. She must have moved to another area altogether if she was not doing the thing she loved doing best. He knew she cared deeply for her parents, now in a care home near North Walsham. Unbelievable, she would have moved far away from them. The disappointment took all the joy of the concert away. He got up and left, deciding he would get back home, pack and go to the farm. He failed to see the lady who quietly slid into her place at the last minute after making sure he had left the church.

The tea things had been cleared away. Until then there had been the usual exchange of the week's happenings. "I thought you went up the city to see some sort of concert, lad?" Tom asked enquiringly.

Nick fidgeted with a fork he hadn't needed and decided honesty was the best policy. "Well, I really didn't want to fill in the afternoon with the castle visit and the concert programme looked a bit too varied for me. I really only wanted to see if Jane was there. I've been trying to contact her since I came back from Poland. She…she's disappeared and left no trace. Nobody seems to know where she is."

There was a longish pause while Tom and Emma looked at him. "Any particular reason, lad?" Nick's face gave away the whole reason to them. They both nodded.

Emma said gently, recognising her love-sick grandson, "It just happens sometimes. It'll go in its own good time."

Nick was halfway between misery and anger. "No! Of course, it won't. It's deep. It…It's so deep it can only happen once for me." There was a brief pause.

Changing the subject abruptly, Tom said firmly, "I and Barry had a long talk. He reckons like I do we'd be taking a big risk with that lass in the home. I need to know two things first. If, and I says if, she and the kids come, what happens when we need the bungalow? It's an agricultural one and can't be rented for any other purpose. We might need it. Second, like, it's sort of furnished. Who's going to pay if it's wrecked?"

Nick polled himself back to the new subject. He had fully anticipated these questions. "First one," he answered decisively, "she's on the waiting list for social housing so it won't be permanent anyway. Should you want it before, then I'll find her a holiday flat or house and pay for it. Secondly, any damage or expense is on my account. I'm still living free and can well afford it. So far I haven't actually met her. I'll know more when I have. And, another point, if it doesn't work out within a couple of weeks, I'll move her on. That's a promise." He hesitated. "It's also possible she may not even want to come."

Tom surveyed him steadily for a while. "OK, then lad, we'll give it a try. Seems to us you're making too much of it and should best sit back."

Nick answered fiercely, "No!" He felt really angry, got up abruptly and started to stack the dishwasher.

Tom spoke in a conciliatory way to Nick's back. "Right, then lad, we'll wait till you have. Then if it looks right, we'll think again. Should be possible."

It was three days before Mrs Palmer rang back to tell Nick Christine would like to meet him. Could she bring her about six o'clock when she was sure he would be finished for the evening? She would be sitting in, just in case Christine became unhappy. Nick had no problem with that. So unlikely, he would finish on time, and he changed the last appointment slot and worked through lunch. All day he had to force himself to concentrate and by six o'clock, he was distinctly agitated. Was it possible his grandparents were right after all? Perhaps he was just interfering where he wasn't wanted.

He walked into the waiting room with his eyes shut, called them, and hurried back to his room. Mrs Palmer followed at a brisk pace with Chrissy some way behind. Nick was standing behind his desk with his eyes fixed on the door. She was so small! He couldn't believe he had thought her big and solid. However, her well-remembered cheeky smile spread across her face. Her mouth then opened wide, equally surprised by his appearance. For a full minute, they just stared at each other. Nick could not utter a word of his prepared introduction. His mouth had become so dry, his thoughts full of unwanted memories. Eventually, it was Chrissy who broke the silence. "Christ! Nick, you've bleeding well grown into a beanpole!" Slightly taken aback by the expletive and her coarse accent, he grinned back, not quite knowing what to say. She giggled. "Ar, come off it Nick, 'ave yer gorn so bloody posh yer forgotten how ter speak? Thought it'd a bin me scared 'o you. You bein' a doctor but I 'ain't. I reckon you're more scared o' me." This time it was he who started laughing, a real deep, cleansing laugh. She had obviously gone to a lot of trouble to look her best. Her unruly hair still hung down to her shoulders. No longer the jet black he remembered but heavily streaked with grey. Still curly and all over the place. Her brown eyes were not as full of mischief as they used to be. There was something very worn and sad reminding him of a much older person. She was so much slimmer than he remembered and had dressed carefully in a denim skirt and silky white blouse.

Eventually, Nick found some words. Not the ones he had planned over and over again. But with a smile on his face, he spoke warmly, "Chrissy, it's wonderful to see you. Now, at last, I've a chance to say thank you. Do you remember how you looked after me? Where did you think I'd have been now if you hadn't?"

Chrissy interrupted his flow, excitedly, "In bloody prison, the way you was going. Guessed when you were dragged away from me in that car, yer'd just run and get in with that mob again. What the hell hold had they on yer?"

He thought for a moment. What did they have? He answered slowly, "Not a lot. Just you didn't walk out on that gang unless you wanted to be beaten up. One kid was beaten up in front of me. I never saw him again. I reckon I was both scared stupid and proud of belonging to something. You were a bit like a mum to me; first person who'd shown me any affection since I was dumped back at the home after my foster mum died. You've been in my thoughts, I suppose most days since, as well as other things that still give me nightmares and keep me awake at nights."

Chrissy broke in, "Yeh, that beast. I still wake up screaming my head off thinking he's at it again." For a long couple of minutes, they looked at each other. Mrs Palmer tried to fade into the background knowing they both might find some relief in sharing such terrible memories. Chrissy continued, "Yeh, knew he did the boys first before he came to me? Wasn't strong enough to stop him. He stank and was horrible and filthy. Knew he got me preggers?" Nick shook his head. "Yeh, well, had to tell someone. Told Matron before lots of times before what 'e was like but she kept telling me not to be disgusting. She thought him all nice and said I just made it all up to get attention. But babies show up, don't they? Any road, 'e's shut up for his natural."

Nick acknowledged this with a grin. "Where's the child now? Must be all of 16?"

Her face dropped. "Yeh. Spastic. Couldn't cope. Goes to see 'im when I can. Not much point really." She shrugged her shoulders. "Got another three now." Her face softened. "Never had much luck with men. Most kids like me left on the streets with nowhere to go, the perps get hold of 'em. Puts yer on the game or knocks yer about. Last one near killed me. He'll go down for his natural too, I 'opes. Slimy bugger might get orf. Made his pile using kids." Nick tried not to look horrified at the calm way she was relating all this. He knew it went on all the time but not to his Christine. Christine, who had cared so much for him, didn't deserve any of it. The story was worse than he'd feared.

"Mother no help then?" he asked not expecting to hear anything better.

Chrissy yelled, "Er! Bloody 'ell! She kicked me and Jason out and I ain't seen her again. Moved out. No idea where."

Nick felt his stomach getting knotted. "I watched you for a long time from the window of the nursing home. I couldn't see the kids clearly but you seemed happy with them?"

For the second time, her face softened. "Do yer know, Nick, this is the first time in all them years I've been playing with them properly like? Usually been scared, he'd bash 'em up too. Always said 'e would if I didn't do what 'e said. This is the 'appiest I've ever been."

"Look, Chrissy," Nick said hurriedly, determined this time he would get out exactly what he wanted to say, "my grandparents have an empty bungalow on the farm. Not sure it's got enough beds but it's got enough furniture and it will be standing empty. They say you can have it while you're waiting for accommodation. It's free. Won't cost you. Kids can stay at the same school. How about it?"

She looked at Nick, open mouthed. For the first time, Chrissy looked over to Mrs Palmer and addressed her. "How d'yer feel about that Mrs P? Give yer an extra room an' it's a bit crowded with the four of us?"

Mrs Palmer answered very calmly, "It's up to you, Christine. It's way out in the country. You've never experienced that. Quiet. No street lights. Smelly cows and sheep. Have to mind your language a bit. However, you might be glad of the space and a house to look after."

Chrissy's face lit up. "Do yer know? It'll be the first time in my life I've 'ad a home of my own! Yeh, I'd love it. Now, Nicky, I want to 'ear about yer."

Chapter 26
Time with Yuri

Nick delivered Chrissy and the three girls the following Saturday. Pathetically, the whole of their worldly goods was in one small suitcase. How she had kept the three girls so clean and tidy he could not imagine. Chrissy had done a quick food shop. He guessed she had not realised there was no nipping down to buy the forgotten items.

He shouldn't have been surprised. The beds were made, including an extra folding one. The kitchen cupboards looked full of essential foods. The table was laid and a large cottage pie and a plum crumble were sitting on the table just needing to be warmed up. Emma was sitting on one of the kitchen chairs as they came in. The children looked around in awe. Chrissy took one look at it all and burst into floods of tears. Emma got up and went quietly over to her and enveloped her in her arms until the sobs subsided. She handed Chrissy a couple of sheets of kitchen roll. She turned to the children who had looked worriedly at their mother. "Your mam is happy, now. That's why she was crying."

She gave them her warm smile and the gentle Norfolk voice made them try to smile back. "Now," she said briskly, "I need to know your names."

They stood woodenly in front of her. "I'm June and I'm ten."

"That's right, nice name. Guess your birthday is in June?" June nodded energetically. Her long frizzy black hair went all over her thin face.

"And I'm April cos my birthday is in April." Piped up the youngest. "And I'm going to be five." She was fairer than her sisters but had the same brown eyes.

"Well, what about you?" asked Emma gently of the middle girl who had drawn back.

Eventually, she whispered, "I'm Lulu," and hid behind June. She was different from the other two. Her hair was straight and her features very Asian.

After they had finished a tour of the bungalow with the girls shrieking for joy as they found there was a bed for each of them, and there was a shower room as well as a bathroom, Nick showed them the garden which still had a swing in it. He'd tested it and knew it was safe. He left them exploring while he and Emma wandered back to his grandparents' cottage. "Do you know," Emma said tearfully, "they haven't had a single toy between them, not even a cuddly toy. In that case she brought there were just their clean school clothes and night dresses. All terribly worn but clean and ironed. I didn't see what was in the toilet bag but I'm glad I found some towels."

They walked the rest of the way in silence. As they sat down to tea, Nick said thoughtfully, "Gran, if you write out a list of what needs to be got, I'll make time to shop on Monday. Have they got the right clothes for Mersham primary school?"

Emma plonked his tea down in front of him. "Don't be silly, Nick, that girl's got gumption and pride. Let me handle this. I could do with some help in the house and Barry's lot certainly could. She'll need something to do and we can pay her. Anyway, I'll be taking them to school on Monday."

Nick looked at Emma open mouthed. "But…but…" he tailed off.

She looked him straight in the eye. "I know I haven't driven for years because Tom always does it. But I can and I will. That girl needs help."

As Nick drove back on Sunday evening, he had a comfortable feeling Emma had found a mission in life, and Chrissy had found a place to be. He had to make sure she had somewhere permanent to live. Chrissy had looked blankly at them on the Sunday morning when they went off to their different churches but apart from that, all seemed well. It would be nearly a fortnight before he could be back. The following weekend he had two eight-hour sessions working for the co-operative out of hours cover.

Above all, he so longed to tell Jane what was happening. There was so much to tell her and he had no idea where she was. He couldn't think of what else to do to find her.

He also very much wanted to visit Yuri and Maria. He had been very disturbed by her last report on his health. The schedule had listed Maria as on duty for one of the eight-hour sessions but she had asked him if he would mind covering it for her. That was so unlike her he thought there must have been yet more of a deterioration. His preoccupation with Jane and now Chrissy had made him almost forget everything and everybody else. He hadn't visited for too long.

His plan to visit Yuri was brought forward on Monday morning by Maria catching him on the way in and inviting him for tea that evening. Not that unusual but Nick was now more worried than ever. He was even more concerned by her next request. "Nick, I need to pop home mid-morning but I'm on-call. Please would you cover for me?" He agreed readily but when he got time to think, he felt more apprehensive. He managed to catch Charles during coffee break, even though he was running behind as usual.

"Yes, Nick," he said seriously as he got up, "I've been going in two or three times a week recently. His chest is still not too good, and he's so thin now there's almost nothing of him. Maria's got it in perspective and expecting the worst. Her mum's coming to stay as soon as she can, to give a hand with the children."

It was a glorious evening, and to his surprise, Yuri was in the conservatory tucked into his special chair. Despite the warmth of the day, he was smothered in soft woolly rugs. Nick drew a chair up alongside. "Well, Yuri," he asked, "what are you up to?"

Yuri peered up at him with his infectious smile. "Nikolaus! How good it is to see you." Yuri's voice was barely above a whisper. His breathing was erratic and laboured. "Nikolaus, listen, I'm not going to be here much longer." There was a long pause while Nick waited for him to continue. "I am only now a burden. To Maria and myself. Time to go. Before I go Nikolaus, go and look in my desk." Another long pause while he recovered any breath he could find. "In my room. Third one down on the right. An envelope for you. Look." Nick rose slowly and did as he was told. He could hear Maria and the children chatting happily in the kitchen. Tea smelt wonderful. Thyme or rosemary or other herbs. Very French. Having retrieved the large envelope, with Polish stamps, he went back to sit by Yuri. Yuri smiled.

"Open it, Nikolaus, open it." Inside were several thick, folded plans. Puzzled, Nick spread them out and gradually a huge smile spread over his face. "I design a house for you. I get my architect brother to draw it up. Eh?"

For five minutes, Nick silently examined the contents. "Yuri, this is so wonderful. It shall be built. I have never had such a happy present. I can't think of a better way of saying it." A shadow suddenly cast over his face, and the sudden tears almost fell. Without Jane, there would be no point in building anything.

"Nikolaus, Nikolaus. Stop. I see you're hurt. She's waiting for you. I know. I know."

Nick refrained from raising his voice above a whisper. "Do you, do you Yuri, know something I don't?"

Yuri shut his eyes and said wearily, "I say too much." He opened his eyes again. "Nikolaus. You take her to Poland to see my brothers? You promise? You loved it too?" Dumbly, Nick nodded his assent. Maria called; it was time to eat. Choked, he came into the kitchen. The children happily grabbed his full attention with all their news.

When it was almost bedtime Sophia said calmly to Nick, "You do know our daddy is on his way to heaven, don't you? Soon we won't see him anymore. It will be terribly sad." With that, she ran off.

When the children and Yuri had been put to bed, Maria and Nick sat in the conservatory watching the evening sun as they drank their coffee. "I think we're into the last few weeks of having Yuri with us," she said. "It's going to be tough but my mother is coming to help hold us up."

Nick nodded. "I am so touched by the plans for my new house. Bedrooms labelled 'child one, child two and child three'. I…I had so hoped to be able to think of a home with someone I love but it's too late, I think. She's gone. I just cannot imagine loving anyone else, ever." Maria remained silent. Nick felt he could not ask her directly. "I have promised Yuri I will visit Poland again. I will love to do that and explore Krakow more. There is so much to see there." He had made a promise to revisit Krakow. With Jane. He had to fulfil that promise.

Maria waited a few moments before asking, "Nick, have you done anything about seeing the psychologist yet?"

Nick shook his head rapidly. "No, and I'm glad I haven't. Chrissy and I have been over the ground for both of us. I have someone now who knows all about the horrors we went through. Just talking about it puts it back in the box, knowing if either of us has a problem we can explore it with each other. I'm even sleeping properly. It's like having a real sister."

Rather diffidently, she asked, "Do you think you are getting fond of her?"

Nick replied crossly, "No, of course not. You're the second person to suggest that. It would be impossible for two damaged people to get together in any sort of way, other than a brother, sister one. Absolutely not. There is someone much more important in my life but I've got to find her."

Chapter 27
A Happy Chrissy and a Funeral

Tentatively ten days later, Nick drove back to the farm. A few phone calls during the interval had not given him much indication of how things were going. "Just fine!" was about the most sensible answer to his questions. It was a glorious summer evening and tea was going to be late. Nick seized the opportunity to walk across to find Chrissy and see for himself how things were. With his heart thumping, he couldn't find her in the bungalow. He wandered into the farmyard itself. The cows were just going back into the field after milking and he heard someone singing. It was Chrissy! Wearing a brown warehouse overall held up with string, she was busily cleaning out the milking parlour very energetically. She stopped as she saw Nick approach and she heard him draw breath. "Cor, Nick!" she exclaimed. "I ain't enjoyed anything so much. Them cows. I loves 'em. I'm learnin' how ter manage the machines. And I'm cleanin' for yer gran, and I'm 'elping Brenda with the kids. Nick, I'm earning dosh. Never, ever 'ad a penny of me own."

Now completely baffled by events, he asked hesitantly, "Where're the kids?"

"Oh, them, they're with Spooky."

Taken aback, he asked, "Who, or what is 'Spooky'?"

She shrugged. "I dunno. Just Spooky. Him, that does the cows. They're 'elping with them calves, I guess." With that, the new stockman, having overheard voices, came around the corner. He grinned at Nick. Tall, skeletally thin but wiry.

"Hi," he said, "I'm Spooky. Rather like it."

Even more bemused now, Nick was beginning to feel amused by the whole situation. "Well, I guess," Nick replied, "you have another name somewhere but why 'Spooky'?"

Spooky replied in his rather jerky speech which was northern, definitely not Norfolk, "Came and found kids around a dead pigeon. Poking it. Making a proper examination of it. Frightened the life out of 'em, I did, so they christened me 'Spooky'." With his unshaven chin, long salt and pepper straggly hair sticking out from his cap, along with his slightly forbidding expression, it suited him well.

Just then Nick's cousin, Barry, came up behind him thumping him hard on the back. "Well, Nick, lad, it's a first. You've actually done something to keep the farm going instead of swanning it around in Mersham. That girl over there" – he pointed a finger at Chrissy – "is a natural. After a week, knew every cow. All 60 of 'em. Put the milkers on. Spotted a sore teat I'd missed. And reckons she'll stay. Had almost decided to give over to just sheep but if she works out to help Kev, here, I'll get back to the 120 head for good."

Utterly surprised by now, almost doubting what he was hearing, Nick turned to Chrissy who was grinning at him while leaning on the vast broom. "Didn't know I'd got it in me, did yer Nicky? Thought I was a right townie. I've never bin so 'appy in all my life."

Nick shook his head. "Be real, Chrissy, you've never even been in the country before. In the winter it's, cold, muddy and double the work. I do know, I get roped in at lambing time." She continued to grin at him.

At that moment, the children came rushing around shouting for Spooky. "We've finished. We've done 'em all." This was June who got there first with April close behind.

Spooky looked beyond them. "Ah, Lulu" – who was bringing up the rear – "did you manage to get some milk down the littl'un?"

A radiant smile spread across her face. She nodded. "All of it!"

Spooky gave her the thumbs-up sign and another smile. "She's another natural," he added, "the calves all go to her." All three girls were covered in farmyard dirt but so happy. Nick turned to go. Chrissy leant her broom against a rail and came over to Nick, reached up, and gave him a huge kiss on the cheek whilst leaning away to avoid getting his pristine jeans dirty.

As he turned, he saw a figure in the distance observing the happenings in front of the cowshed. For a full second, Nick hesitated, then ran. He was sure it was Jane. She was fast and had a big head start on him. Her car was parked on the hard standing. She was in and driving off before he could reach her. He banged on the rear window as she sped out of reach.

The next two weeks were particularly busy with extra tourist problems and a summer flu. Yuri was nearing the end. He died quietly in the conservatory surrounded by his plants. Meanwhile, the practice was covering as much of Maria's work as it could. She needed time with the children.

He was buried in the morning with just Maria and the three brothers present. Her mother had taken the children out to an ice cream parlour. The thanksgiving service was in the afternoon in the Roman Catholic Church in the Overstrand Road, near the Cromer Golf Club.

Nick arrived as early as he dared. He was convinced Jane would come. The death had been put in the Times, the Telegraph and the Eastern Daily Press. She had been very close to Maria and had often had the children. He was busy scanning every person who came in when Sophia came and found him. "Nick, Nick, Mummy asks if you will come and sit with Daddy's brothers. They're finding English hard, and are used to you." She grabbed his hand and led him firmly to the pew immediately behind Maria, her mother and the children. Nick did his best not to look embarrassed as he pushed his way along, nor to feel frustration at losing any chance of seeing Jane. His hand was shaken over and over again by the brothers as their tears flowed. Nick couldn't think of the right words, so he just nodded and sat down. He was amazed at the composure of the girls. Sophia turned around several times during the unfamiliar service to make sure he was alright.

The church was packed. As he walked up the aisle with the brothers, he tried to see where Jane was but there was no chance. He had not expected to be invited to the tea in the Golf Club afterwards but was given little choice. The brothers were keen to relive Nick's time there and were busy planning his next visit. Yuri had promised him it would be with Jane.

Chapter 28
Finding

The following Saturday Nick succeeded in getting to his twice-postponed organ lesson. For the first time on the principal organ. He eagerly followed Richard up the open spiral staircase to find the organ loft. It was surprisingly spacious with a magnificent view of the church interior. The organ with its four manuals, pre-planned pedal stops and numerous eye-level ones was daunting. Richard suggested he heard the Bach Prelude and Fugue Nick had prepared. But first offered his help in choosing the stops.

Nick was gradually getting more depressed with his inability to find any trace of Jane but just for that hour, he felt like a king playing this magnificent organ. Finally, he was given a piece of sight-reading. A thing Richard liked to do at the end of each lesson. It was fairly easy. Nick chose appropriate stops, having listened carefully to Richard and executed it very happily and correctly. He got down from the stool, took his music ready to put in his music case. A voice from below shouted, "Richard, have you finished, can I come to get that piece of Telemann you promised me?"

Richard leant over the stairs. "Got it. Come on up." Nick was packing his music case with his back to Richard. Turning to go, he saw who it was. Paralysed, he stood staring at her with his mouth open. She, too, unable to speak stood staring back. Richard sat on the stool looking patiently from one to another.

"Jane, Jane." Nick was so hoarse he could not continue. All he wanted to do was to envelop her in his arms. He took a step nearer but she took one back and put her hand up in front of her.

There they remained for some minutes until suddenly brought back to earth by Richard saying in his very stilted, prosaic way, "If you two have stopped staring at each other, I'd quite like to go and get some lunch." He held out a folder of music to Jane, slightly amused by the situation. "If this is what you came for, then here it is." She took it with one hand without looking at him. Richard moved behind Nick, giving him a gentle push towards the spiral staircase. Jane followed slowly. Nick was not prepared to let her get away. He reached out and held her firmly by the arm and drew her away from the foot of the stairs enabling Richard to escape. As far as they were concerned, there was no one else in the vast church. Several visitors turned to stare at them. Nick struggled for words. When they came, she could barely hear them.

"Jane...Jane...don't leave me again, please...please stay with me. I can't bear it. I've searched everywhere for you. Why, Jane, why? What have I done?" Still she said nothing, just kept looking at him in a way he couldn't grasp. "Jane." Nick tried to go on. "Jane, I love you with all I am. If...if...if you feel nothing for me, tell me. I...I don't know what I'll do but at least I would know."

Jane gently moved Nick's hand away from her arm. He stepped back. She found her voice, high and trembling. "Nick,

I do care but you don't know why I can't. Why you must go away and forget me. I moved to get out of your way. I felt, I feel too much for you. I had to come and see you when you didn't know I was there. Several times. You nearly walked into me once and saw me at the farm." Her eyes filled with tears. Stunned by the thought that anything she could have done could mar his love for her; he sought for a way of saying it.

Pleadingly, almost in tears himself, he said quietly, "Jane, there is nothing in the whole wide world you could possibly have done which could dent my love for you, not by one iota."

Miserably, trying to restrain the tears, she shook her head. "There is." The tears were now flowing freely. Nick stepped forwards again and took her in his arms. She unwillingly relaxed, and put her head on his shoulder and wept freely. One of the sightseers who was walking past asked if they were alright. Nick lifted his head and nodded. He'd found Jane. He had to find her problem.

"Jane, darling Jane, we've got to sort this out. But not now. It's too public." Where, where in the city was there somewhere private? He racked his brains. No, they needed to do this now. He led her to the small chapel in the north transept. They would hopefully be left alone there.

They sat side by side, Jane looked straight ahead. Nick feasted his eyes on her. After a couple of minutes, Nick could wait no longer. He burst out. "Jane, please look at me, I've a lot to tell you. Please, please Jane. But I must know first what is wrong. Is it something I've done?" He had planned this little speech almost every night and at long, long last had managed to get the words out. Pleadingly, reaching out a hand to her, he tried to force her to look at him. She pushed his hand away.

Eventually, Jane spoke but still gazing rigidly straight ahead. "You must understand, Nick, it is a foul story. When I have told you all, I can promise you will only want to walk away from tatty second-hand goods." She had stopped crying, now just looked sad.

Nick said impulsively, "Jane, there is nothing, however bad could stop me loving you. I promise."

After a short while, Jane gulped and spoke in almost a whisper, "I have spoken to nobody ever about it. Emma and Maria think I left because they could see you were besotted with me and I was not with you. Not true. I am, was." Here she paused, gathering courage to go on. She took a quick glance at Nick, then looked away, speaking decisively in that low, hoarse voice. "The answer will still be a 'No', Nick. I mean it. No, no, no. But OK, if you really insist on hearing why, here goes." She swallowed hard. "I was brought up very strictly as you may have gathered. Very loving parents who were perhaps a bit too strict. My social life was limited to chapel activities. My choice of school friends were not made particularly welcome. University was an eye-opener. I met boys for the first time. Boys who just wanted to take girls to bed. Of course, I knew all about it but didn't think I ever could. I'd virtually never drink alcohol and never dreamt of taking drugs. Definitely no plans to lose my virginity before meeting the right person. A bit lonely, homesick, I suppose, I got caught up in it all. The night it happened was a closed book. I knew nothing about it until that is, I woke up in the morning in a strange accommodation bed in a different part of the campus with this boy trying it on again. I've no memory of how I reacted. I could not believe it had happened to me."

She stopped, waiting for Nick to speak. "Jane, darling Jane, if that is all, then you could tell anyone you loved about that. Those who know you even a tiny bit would never hold that against you. You were a victim." Jane still did not move.

Eventually, she drew a deep breath and continued in a flat voice, "There is much more. It never happened again that way. I have never touched alcohol since. I became a loner. Drugs obviously never. My relief was huge when I found I was not pregnant. But that was not the end. If it had been, I could have somehow lived with it." She stopped. Nick sat absolutely still; aware the real revelation was to come. He gazed unseeingly into the distance trying to imagine anything that could be so awful. Eventually, she did continue in the same monotone. "Popped into my pigeon-hole was an envelope. It contained photographs of the night of which I had no memory. So utterly shocking I still feel sick. There is no doubt they are of me. The note that accompanied stated he would expect similar rewards or they would be sent to everyone he could think of, including my parents. I really had no choice but to comply. Even if I got the authorities on to him, he would still have the photos and would still send them. He wouldn't be bothered by the prosecution. He got his kicks. A year later, I met Robin and really fell in love. He had also had a bit of a wild time. He did not expect a virgin. Yes, we had sex long before we married but we were both very sure of each other. This rat of a man gloated and made use of it. I'm almost certain Emily is Robin's daughter but would never dare to have it tested. Once married, it seemed to stop. We all scattered after our degrees and I guess he either moved a long way away or lost track of me. Possibly the threat to tell my parents was imaginary. I cannot see how he could know their address. Then, just as I dreamt you and I could make some sort of future together, he turned up on my doorstep. It was a week before you were due to go to Poland. That day, fortunately, I had the garage people there as my car had died and I wanted a replacement. Also, Emily was there. The thought terrified me of what he might do to her or she could find out..." She tailed off, barely finding the words to continue. "I panicked. Managed to finish the car transaction and asked them to deliver Emily, a quickly packed suitcase and myself to Maria's home."

Nick broke an, furiously angry, "What a disgusting member of the human race. He doesn't belong there. He needs to be locked up forever. Nothing to do with you. I'd...I'd like to throttle him. We'll find him and deal with him forever." He turned to her, trying to get her to respond. After a long silence, speaking very quietly now, he asked. "How much did you need to tell Maria?"

Jane lifted her head. "Not much. One doesn't need to with her. But there was no way she could have realised the full extent of my terrors. She just calmly made up a couple of beds and invited us to stay. Then later to find a place to rent near Norwich."

Nick, appalled, thought hard. "Any idea of this rat's name?" Jane shook her head. "Have you ever tried to find out?"

"No." Jane again swallowed hard. "How could I? I have no idea how to start."

Angrily, Nick replied, "I don't either. First of all, we'll find that out. The only people now for you to worry about are your parents, if indeed he really does know their address. I think that's unlikely as I believe they have moved a couple of

204

times since then. Wasn't it last year they moved to that retirement village?" She nodded dumbly. "Well, let him get on with it. Times have moved on and can you really think of anyone who would be badly shocked? A few lecturers, the Dean but I guess they've all met it before. And how much about you does this rat really know?"

Jane gasped. "But Nick, it's not as simple as that. It isn't. And you. How would you feel if they landed in your in-tray and the whole surgery found out?"

He answered very steadily. "It would not affect me one bit. It's you I've fallen in love with. Not your past. And the rest of the surgery? I guess whoever opened it would make damn sure it went no further. Besides, it's now commonplace. And as I said, most of us have seen it all before." He was now beginning to see a ray of hope for Jane and himself. "I think the only important thing now is to try and finish him off. You won't be his only victim. By a long chalk. I have both pleasant and unpleasant experiences of the police but I can think of a really helpful sergeant who might know what to do. Shall we ask him?

There was no answer for so long that Nick thought she had fallen asleep. Then she spoke more normally, "Please would you? I mean, find out how to start, if anything can be done, that is. It might help someone else. Meanwhile, Nick, that is by no means all. There is worse to come."

Nick got up, stood in front of her, speaking rapidly, "Jane, there can't be. Please, tell me we can love each other with no past between us?"

She put her hands up forcing him to step back. In a controlled voice, she went on, ignoring his interruption, "This is even more important to me. I loved Robin so much. It was fine until we married. Then everything changed. He was, in modern terms, controlling. My life was managed, supposedly in a very loving Biblical way, for 24 hours a day. The day he died we had our first and only row. About money. He was spending more than we had, or could possibly afford and I couldn't go on seeing it happen. Not with the baby due. I was relieved when he died. Yes, Nick. That is the most terrible thing I've lived with. I've relished my independence and I am desperately afraid of losing it. Now do you see? Go away and just leave me alone."

Open mouthed Nick stared at her. "But…but I would never, ever dream of controlling you. I'm not made that way. It's just not in me. Please, Oh God, please give me a chance."

After an eternity, she replied, "Nick, I will need a month totally away from you. It's not just me, it is Emily as well. I want to have that month to think things over. Before we part today, I need to know what your gremlins were. I will need to absorb those too."

Chapter 29
Nick Interferes

It was another lovely evening on the Friday with the sun low, the sunset beginning to create a scenic wide Norfolk panorama. Back at the farm, Nick got out of his car. For some time, he just wondered at the different colours of the clouds in the sky. Chrissy broke his reverie. She ran towards him, giving him a quick peck on the cheek. "Oi, there Nicky! 'aven't seen yer for a coupla weeks. Orl right?" Did he detect a slight Norfolk inflexion in her speech? Her face was radiant. She had changed into smart jeans with a florid top. June and April came rushing up to Nick jumping up and hugging him in their filthy outfits. Lulu trailed behind but Nick made sure she got a hug too. It was nothing like as spontaneous as the other two. For the umpteenth time, Nick resolved to find out why. Now was not the moment.

"Looks as if you are doing well!" He grinned. "How did you survive the deluge earlier in the week? Bet it gave you a taste of what winter will be like."

She laughed. "Yeh, well. It were right mess 'ere. Bit of a flood like. Needed two showers meself that day, as well as the one outside. Stop that worryin' Nicky, we're the 'appiest ever. All of us." Nick raised an eyebrow. Lulu was wandering off on her own again. Something there was not right. Perhaps Gran would know.

Nick had got into the habit of starting his weekend in the farm late on the Friday after tea. This time he decided he would only brood if he stayed in his flat. Emma fortunately had ham, and along with a couple of eggs and chips he enjoyed an unhealthy meal. Emma asked tentatively, "Now, lad, how be things between you and Jane then?" He was immediately aware the grapevine had enlightened Emma, and probably Maria, of their meeting. Having guessed this would happen, and expecting this question, he was prepared.

"Sort of hopeful. We're taking a month to work out personal problems. We've promised not to contact each other. It's so hard." He stopped there abruptly. "Gran, why did you refuse to let me know you were in contact with Jane? I'd have not been needlessly unhappy if I'd just had a word to know she was safe."

Emma spoke through closed lips. "If I make a promise, I keeps it."

She was about to get up but Nick changed the subject. "Gran, do you know why Lulu is so reserved? It seems unnatural."

Emma sat down again looking a bit dejected. "Not really, like. But I did ask and she did tell me it was him what took a dislike to her. Guess, with her story, he bashed the kid up too." He resolved to get whole thing sorted out with Chrissy. That child needed help.

A few days later when Nick decided there was time in a very busy day to whip out and find a sandwich for lunch, his mobile rang. Chrissy sounded frantic. "Nicky, school's just rung and says Lulu's bin sick and looks poorly. There ain't no

208

one 'ere with a car. Can you 'ave 'er for a bit?" There didn't seem to be a choice. Lulu, or a sandwich. The school had got used to him collecting and delivering the children. They would gladly release her to his care. He took the car around in case she was too weak to walk. Anyway, he needed to get her back to Chrissy's care. He hadn't expected to see her looking quite so poorly. When he saw, he changed his plans. It was a short trip back to the surgery. He picked her up and laid her gently on the couch. She had been cleaned up but still stank of sick.

"Does your tummy hurt?" Nick asked gently. She had curled up into a ball. She pointed at her tummy button. "Lulu, I'm going to ask you to lie out straight for a minute." Pressing her tummy very gently, he found a tender spot down on the lower right, so tender that she cried out and tried to vomit again. He had a hasty debate with himself. He couldn't send her alone in an ambulance. She needed her appendix removed urgently. There wasn't time to go and fetch Chrissy. That would take all of an hour or more. He told Lulu to stay put and not to move. Rushing out to find Maria or Charles or any doctor free, he bumped into the locum who was still filling Penny's slot. "Are you frantic this afternoon?" he asked.

"Actually not." She shook her head and looked at him in surprise. "I'm on supervision mainly, and life is fairly quiet. Why?"

"A child I feel responsible for has a very acute appendix and I'd like to get her to the N and N soonest. I'll get the paramedic to drive, if I can find him. And phone her mother to get there asap." As he was dashing off, she shouted after him, "He's just grabbing some lunch in the coffee place. Let me go and get him." Nick went back to Lulu, picked her up and gently carried her to the paramedic's car outside. He cradled her all the way to the hospital while making phone calls to Chrissy, Emma, Barry and the hospital. He then spoke to Lulu. "Lulu, listen to me. You'll have gathered from the phone calls you have a problem. Do you know what a boil looks like? All yellow and painful?" There was a little nod, so he went on. "You've got one inside your tummy. It's got to come out or it might pop in your tummy. The only way to do it is to make a small hole and drag it out. You'll be fine in a couple of days. You will be fast asleep when they do it. Mummy is coming to the hospital to meet you. Do you understand, Lulu, what I'm saying?"

A small voice asked in misery, "Will it take the pain away? It hurts."

Nick replied very reassuringly, "Yes. It'll be a bit sore for a day or two when you wake up, and you may need a further couple of days off before." By the time he got back to the surgery, most of his patients had either been seen or re-booked. He decided to try his luck with the school. Correctly, he should have asked Chrissy's permission first but as Lulu's doctor, he thought they might be willing to talk to him. The secretary, who he knew him well, assured him the head would be only too delighted to have a chat about Lulu.

He was surprised by how young Mrs Rushmer was. Possibly 35 but no older. Beautifully cut fairly short brown hair, light brown eyes in a heart-shaped face, she exuded efficiency. Her crisp linen navy dress with a necklace of blue and white beads sat well on her. She stood up as he entered and gestured to the seat opposite her. "I'm intrigued by your wanting to discuss Lulu. I've been trying really hard to collar her mother but she seems inaccessible! Hurries back to the car as soon as she sees me or one of the staff approaching." Nick wondered just how much she knew of the past history. "Before I start," she tempered, "how much do you know about her life before she came here?"

Nick sat up straighter. He said abruptly, "Just about everything. Her mother and I spent two years together in an appalling children home. I know a lot about her life of abuse. I found them the bungalow on my grandfather's farm. Enough?"

She relaxed visibly. "Then I feel I can ask a question or two. Does she have access to books? Or writing materials? Or time away from her noisy, mischievous sisters?"

Nick could answer those questions easily. "No, no and no. They've never lived on a farm before. April and June relish the out of doors, like their mother. Lulu patently obviously is less happy with it. I do know. I grew up there and it was not for me. She loves the poor animals and is very patient with them. Mother, I would guess is hugely streetwise, intelligent but possibly illiterate. Schooling there was but terrifying for me, and of no use to her. She had a child before she was 14. She even didn't get up to secondary school with her year as she had missed so much. Does that help?"

"What about her father. Do we know anything about him?"

Nick stalled. "Don't ask. Just think of a possible life-style instead."

Mrs Rushmer nodded slowly. "Only, she's a very unusual child. She caught up her schoolwork in record time. Is already going to be at the head of the class in a few weeks. Her teachers are delighted with her but she won't take books or homework back with her. Why?"

Nick could think of a dozen reasons. "Possibly would cause amusement by her siblings, Mother would tell her not to waste her time, worried books might get damaged or just self-conscious at being 'different'." He tapped the desk thoughtfully. "Leave that one with me. I think I can see a way around. Oh, and by the way, her appendix should be out by now. Poor kid, it was a bad one."

Mrs Rushmer opened her mouth in surprise. "Oh, dear, we thought it was just a tummy bug. They're always doing the rounds."

As Nick got up to leave, he had a thought. "Could you find me a couple of books I could take in to her or give her when she gets home? It would be a good excuse to start a new regime for her."

"Excellent idea! I'll ask her class teacher tomorrow and have them ready for collection at going home time."

It was in fact two days before Lulu could come home. It was mid-afternoon on Saturday when the call came to collect her. The appendix had been badly infected and her temperature had remained high. The ward was full of praise for her. Emma had been driven in by Tom and had sat with her.

Chrissy now had full charge of the milking at weekends and could not be easily spared. Nick was only too happy to help. Lulu greeted him with a real happy smile. She'd already read one of the three books the school had provided. As Emma said, the next stage had to be an introduction to the library in Mersham.

On Saturday, just one week before the date when Nick would get his ultimatum from Jane, he arrived back at the farm earlier than expected. Emma looked up at him in surprise. He grinned at her. "I've decided to take a week off before the holiday season sets in earnest and partners want school time off for summer holidays." He added diffidently, "There are a couple of things I need to sort before, if, when, Jane decides we could, well, get married. I keep telling myself, when. I keep thinking it can't go wrong. Can it?"

Emma looked at him thoughtfully. "I don't rightly know, Nick but Jane's a caring lass and if she'd decided against you, I reckon she'd let you know earliest."

He became aware of open exercise books on the table with pencils and paper strewed all over the place. Emma nodded to a corner armchair by the window. "She's found Harry Potter. Homework can wait. Well into book two now."

Chrissy was fusing around the yard as usual with her back to him. It looked spotless and far too early for milking. "Well, it looks as if you're in control. Where are the kids?"

She turned around to see where he was. "Blimey, you're early! No work today?" Her eyes were checking all along the stalls. "I just likes to see this place all nice and clean before me girls come in."

"Looks good to me!" Nick said. "But not sure the girls, as you put it, really care."

"Gawd, I can see why you never made a farmer!" Chrissy exploded. "They 'ates their food messed up. Or dirt in their hay. They're like 'umans. Now. Nicky, what 'ave yer done with my Lulu? Wanted you on yer own to ask what the 'ell is goin' on?"

Nick had the grace to look shame-faced. He had never told Chrissy about his chat with the headmistress. "After I'd collected Lulu the day her appendix blew up, I went back to tell the headmistress about her operation." Not the complete truth, Nick thought but near enough.

Chrissy said, perceptively, "And thought yer'd find out what our Lulu was like at school, if I know you, Nicky. Yer might a told me. It's me own girl."

Nick could only blush and nod. "You're right. But she seemed so different from the other two. I couldn't make it out."

"Well, yer could a asked!" Chrissy interrupted angrily. Standing as she was in front of a barn filled with new straw bales, with her hair standing out from her head in all directions, an overall tied around her waist with string, she looked exactly like a scarecrow.

Nick tried not to grin. "I couldn't get you on your own was the main reason. Nor could the head. I gather she tried over and over again. But you might or might not like to know you have an exceptionally clever school working daughter. In just these few weeks, she's as clever as any other child in her class despite not doing her homework."

Chrissy, still annoyed with Nick began to sound a bit conciliatory. "Never had any brains in all my life. Not that sort. Don't need 'em. She'll be fine."

Nick changed tack altogether, now he was sounding cross. "Chrissy, listen to me. We're all different. I was very different. They wanted me to take on the farm but I hated it. I wanted to read, to learn and find a different life. Lulu doesn't have to be like you. She's Lulu and her own person. Give her a chance."

Chrissy looked sullen. "God knows who her dad was. Got ter be 'im. Keeps saying she wants ter be a doctor. That's just cos she's been in the 'ospital."

214

Nick shrugged his shoulders. "Maybe she really does. Come on, Chrissy, she's your daughter as well, and it's you who has done an unbelievably good, stunning job of bringing those kids up. They are amazing, wonderful kids. If…if ever I have any, I'd hope to have them like that. You'll be really proud of them all one day. Sorry I trod on your toes but can't you see she's much happier reading Harry Potter than being out here with you and Spooky?"

"Yeah, well but I'd a found out for myself one day if you'd left me alone." She still looked a bit sulky but a bit more thoughtful. "He used to pick on 'er. She'd never cry like the other two. He'd beat the daylights out of 'er sometimes but she never made a sound."

Nick turned to go back to Tom and Emma for his tea muttering, "Poor kid, and poor you. How on earth you've pulled them through that I can't imagine." He hurried away.

Chrissy called him back. "'ang on a mo. Hell, Nicky, don't know how to tell yer this. Spooky's moved in." With that, she fled, leaving Nick staring into space open-mouthed. Then he grinned. Could be for the best.

Chapter 30
A Hopeful Wedding Present

Next morning at the end of breakfast, Tom moved around to sit by Nick. "Well, lad, what do 'e plan for that week's holiday then?"

Nick looked steadily at the table. "It's…it's the week before I make contact with Jane. I don't think she'd have let me go this far if she really was going to refuse me, do you? I asked Gran last night and she agreed with me." Tom gave him a non-committal shrug. "Anyway," Nick continued, "Yuri made some wonderful plans for a house and I want to spend the week looking for somewhere to build it."

He lifted his head to see how Tom felt about it. "Didn't rightly know 'e had any plans! I'd right like to see them if you'd allow?" Nick jumped up and rushed to bring back his much-treasured briefcase. Gladly, he spread them out over the table, excited to share them. Enthusiastically, he took Tom through all the rooms, the perspectives and the drawings.

Suddenly, Tom stood up. "Got half an hour, son?"

Surprised, Nick looked up. "Yeah, of course. What can I do for you?"

Speaking very non-committedly as he got up from the table, Tom said, "Just you come for a ride with me and we'll see."

They drove back into Mersham and out in a westerly direction for a mile or so. Really, a local back road to Morston. Tom then turned right after a few houses appeared on both sides of the road, then right again into a cul-de-sac. All this time in silence. There was space for four houses. One straight ahead and two on the right had recently been built, all very pleasant detached ones in good sized gardens. On the left was a large field extending into the distance. Tom turned off the engine and broke the silence. Nick was beginning to get a glimmer of what this was all about. "Back in the '70s, land were going a bit cheaper like. Were into sheep, then, more 'n they are now. Twenty-acre field. I bought it. A few years ago, Barry decided like he didn't want all 'em sheep. Them houses on t' main road were going up so tried for planning permission. Amazed when I got it for four houses and a three-acre paddock. Sold those three sites on yer right. Kept this left one in case you ever needed a wedding present." Absolutely stunned, it left Nick speechless. Slowly, he got out of the car, climbed over the fence to just be there. It was completely overgrown but it could be his and Jane's. But she hadn't seen the plans and she might not like the site. All the negative thoughts flashed through his mind. His dream was now so real he could not believe Jane would refuse him. He could so clearly them planning, watching their dream house grow, even having a family he knew it had to happen. He came back to earth. But what if she did? He went back and sat beside Tom who had not left the car, just sat watching the various expressions move across Nick's face.

217

"Gramps," Nick eventually managed to get the words out, "I don't know what to say. So perfect. So perfect, if only. It's lovely. I can see the house, angled to the road to catch the sun morning and evening. Best a good way back from the road. Oh Jane! Gramps, do you think she might like it?"

Tom remained expressionless but with a comfortable glow inside. This was what he wanted to see. "Best ask her, son." They drove back in companionable silence.

The rest of the week was spent with builders, mortgage arrangements, collecting brochures of kitchens and bathrooms and even looking at furniture. All the time he could not get rid of the niggling doubts. Surely, she wouldn't let it go on and on if she meant to refuse him? But why not? They had agreed on no decision for a month. On a couple of days, he had stayed at the farm while Tom and Emma had kept him busy with a mass of little jobs needing an able younger person.

Friday proved impossible. It was a drizzly day and perhaps not the one to have chosen for a long walk. Quite deliberately, he left his phone behind, took the car to Wells-next-Sea parked and walked along the coast to Holkham. The sun emerged to dry him off. It was, even in drizzly weather, a beautiful walk through soft sand and pine trees. Hungry now, he found a pub. He ate fish and chips with mushy peas, so reminiscent of holidays with his grandparents in Great Yarmouth. After he had walked back to the coast, taken a quick paddle across to 'the island' and back as the tide was going out it was time to walk back to his flat and his phone to see if Jane had made any arrangements to meet. There was nothing. Could she have forgotten, or should he be the one to make contact? But he couldn't. He had no way of doing so. Perhaps she really would leave it until the last minute. He was desperate to tell her about the house, the building site and how much he loved her.

Nick had a sleepless night. At six o'clock, he could stand it no longer. He got showered and dressed. But it was early. At seven and eight, still nothing. He could hear the florist below moving her plants around for display and chatting to early passers-by. By nine, he was beside himself with worry when his door opened quietly. There she was. She turned, closed the door and said quietly, almost inconsequentially, "I did try the farm first. Emma made me have some breakfast." Nick's heart sank and his mouth dried up. For a few moments, they looked at each other, both absolutely still. "I would have been here at least an hour earlier. But…but I was in such a state Emma said I wasn't fit to drive." Neither of them quite knew what happened but in a mini second, she was in his arms. There they stayed for an eternity.

Postlude
Ten Years Later

An email from Emily Grovenor,

Hi Mom and Daddy Nick,

Sorry haven't phoned but can't find it.

I'm in the flat and have been to the academy today.

London's noisier despite electric cars and the huge inner zone charge. I do so miss Norfolk. Good to have Lulu as a flat share now. She's got a placement with a solicitor here in London if she passes her law exam at the end of the year. She'll get a first easily. And we've got a couple of lads this year. Thought we ought to keep the Norfolks together. Dad, do you remember that lad who stole a tractor in the snow storm? He was my great friend at primary school. He's training at Kew. Gather he hated the farm and his dad, and his mum is suffering with something mental, so he won't go home. Sad but he's brilliant at washing up. So tidy! Eats for England and looks like it. The boys still party and invite us but we prefer not! Lulu has a soul mate she met on her open day. I think f. They play endless chess and I guess that's where she was all summer. Reckon she and Chrissy live in different worlds. It's sad going to the farm now Gramps is in a care home. Miss Gran so much. Makes me cry. All Chrissy can think about are her blessed animals. Pigs now! And April and June are as bad.

Mummy, you're going to be disappointed. I'm giving up singing this year and just concentrating on flute and organ for the next two. The Royal Academy suggested this as I was struggling somewhat. Will tell you who I've got as profs and what we are studying over the phone when I know who. Flute looks busy with orchestra, quartets and band. Can't practice in the flat so stay on. I promise you I will eat properly.

Now, parents, I want to know about home. Is Louise looking after the ponies properly and are they both riding them for me? And are Louise and Charlotte in the same form at Mershams? I know they tried to separate the twins. And I do hope Thomas is happier at school than he was when I left. He seems so tiny to be even going there. And is Dad still overworking? Lovely to hear both Maria's girls are hoping to do medicine after gap years.

Please send an email. I'll stop being so homesick in a few days. I'll have a good search for my phone.

Lots of love
Emily

Email Nick to Emily in reply

Hello Em,

Phone in post. Found under the bed with numerous other items. Phone soonest.

I know the farm's different but it's still home to me. Remember Chrissy got a first with her prize pig and Spooky a second with his heifer in a huge class at the Norfolk and Norwich Show?

It's farm open days this week. April and June are in their element showing schoolchildren around. Gramps is in with a lot of other very elderly Norfolk farmers. A lot never married. They never stop going over their old times together. He fought all the way before going there but is now happy as can be under the circumstances.

Mum, a bit disappointed it was singing you gave up but can see why. She's off singing tonight in a very select Bach group somewhere. Thrilled to be asked.

Twins have been put in the same class at Postams but not allowed to sit by each other. Tommy adjusting slowly to school. Afraid we spoilt him a bit. Your siblings are missing their big sister, massively.

Ponies well used and looked after.

Maria decided to finally retire at Christmas which leaves me the most senior partner in the practice.

Can't think of anything else.

Love
Daddy Nick
Tons of love Ma and Pa XXXX